SHE WHISPERS SWEET

AN ARTEMIS BLYTHE MYSTERY THRILLER

GEORGIA WAGNER

CONTENTS

PROLOGUE

She'd always been terrified of heights, but the weekend of wine-tasting had given her liquid courage, and now, Gina Clarkson leaned against the wooden rail of the villa's balcony, staring out over the mountain pass far below.

What might it be like to fall two-hundred feet from the sheer drop, crashing against those stones far below?

She shivered at the thought, glancing over her shoulder, through the glass, where she could hear sounds in the kitchen from her boyfriend … No, *no,* husband now after yesterday. He was making dinner for the newlyweds.

It had been Ben's idea to rent a villa on the cliff-face for their honeymoon.

Gina took a sip of Sangria, tasting the chilled flavors of citrus and herb, the glass cold against her fingertips as she watched the sun dipping behind the Cascade Mountains, leaving streaks of gold and red along the cliffs and valleys.

And that's when the lights went out.

She hesitated, wrinkling her nose and glancing back at the villa.

The windows were suddenly dark. The distant light of the sun seemed even dimmer now as clouds pulled across the beaming face of the light in the sky.

"Ben?" she called out, turning now.

Her steps were a bit wobbly. She'd had a bit too much to drink, but it was her honeymoon, after all. She deserved a bit of indulgence.

Her lips pressed in a thin line, causing her cheeks to dimple, and she brushed her golden hair from her eyes.

The sounds from the kitchen had faded.

She wrinkled her nose, taking another tottering step forward.

The villa was isolated. The rest of the vineyard was beyond the shadow of the mountain, hidden over the ridge. Her fingers grazed the glass of the patio door as she pushed it slowly open and peered inside.

Inside the villa, a dormant and cold fireplace lay settled off to her right, under a large smart TV. A leather couch with automatic buttons on the side sat in one corner, across from a love-chair that they'd already made good use of.

There was an end table near wooden stairs leading up to the top level and a door leading to the basement, which was unfinished but, judging from the tour they'd been given when they'd first arrived, held a couple of old-fashioned arcade games. For decor more than entertainment according to the hosts of the place.

Now, standing in the main room of the villa, on wooden flooring that matched the walls, her gaze cast about in the dark. The TV had been on earlier, playing a quiet movie of natural beauty. The electric fireplace had also been on.

Now, both were out.

The light from the kitchen was off.

Even the sound of the vent over the stove had gone quiet.

And then she froze.

Something was lying on the floor.

A dark lump by the door.

The front door was open, and a gust of wind whistled through the faint crack.

It took her a second to realize there was a body on the ground, motionless.

Her eyes widened in horror. She dropped the glass.

It shattered at her feet, spitting crystals and droplets of cold liquid across her ankles.

She let out a small yelp then sprinted forward, racing across the slick, wooden ground.

It was darker in the house than on the porch, as some of the curtains were drawn.

She dropped next to the body by the door, her hands reaching out desperately.

"No, no, no!" she was saying. Sometimes, Ben had fainting spells, but it had been nearly a year since his last one. "Where are your meds! Ben, where are they?"

But he didn't reply. She tugged his shoulder, forcing his face to turn towards hers.

For one horrible moment, she didn't recognize the man on the ground.

It wasn't her husband...

No... No, wait.

Her imagination was playing tricks.

His face was streaked in red, though, and his eyes were closed. The combination of the red and the shadows and the effect of her drink had momentarily played a trick on her mind.

His features were rigid, though. Frozen.

Ben didn't look like himself...

And then... as her mind caught up with what she was seeing, she froze.

The red wasn't sauce from the Bolognese he'd been cooking—the fragrant odor she could smell coming from the kitchen—nor was it some trick of the light in the dark villa.

Blood.

Streaming down the side of his face, staining his cheek. Droplets of crimson clung to his fluttering eyelashes.

"Benny!" she screamed now, horror filling her.

And then she spotted the thick branch by the door. A branch that looked as if it had been dragged in from the trees adorning the mountains. A thick, hefty branch—more like a club.

The front door was open.

A club on the ground.

Ben, lying in a pool of his own blood, and the two of them isolated in the mountains.

It took a few seconds for her Sangria-affected mind to piece together the information, but once she did, her eyes widened in terror.

Someone was in the cabin with them.

She whirled around, heart pounding a million miles a minute.

"Ben, please, get up! Are you okay?" she cried, desperate.

She looked around the dark spaces, listening intently. She shot a quick look towards the door. Still open.

What if the person was outside?

Who was it?

Was she just imagining things?

Chills erupted down her spine as she reached out and slammed the door. Just in case.

She locked it then hooked the chain on the door.

And that's when she heard a creaking sound. Coming from above...

Was that the old window that hadn't latched last night?

Shit... Shit... Shit...

If someone was upstairs already—if they'd struck Ben then snuck past...

She stared towards the stairwell, but the shadows remained dormant. No motion.

She tried to tug at her husband, to get him to rise, but he was unconscious.

She began pulling him, trying to drag him to the basement. But he'd once been a football player, and he still had that workout habit. Too large—too muscled for her to carry.

"Shit," she whispered to herself. "SHIT!"

She hastened to the kitchen, snatching a cutting knife from where her husband had been chopping onions. The effect of the onions caused her eyes to sting then begin to water.

Gripping the knife, she whirled around...

Still no sound.

Her other hand was fumbling in her pocket, almost as if of its own volition.

Where was her damn phone! She needed to call for the police. Would there be reception up here?

She shivered now, staring towards the stairwell again. She'd left her phone in the basement in an old wicker basket. She bit her lip, cursing inwardly that she'd ever agreed to the no-phones bet with Ben for the weekend.

She gripped the knife, glancing back at her husband where he lay motionless on the ground.

She couldn't leave him. What if the intruder came back?

Was there even an intruder?

How else would her husband have been struck? The door was open...

Yes. Someone was here.

But maybe they'd already left? Stolen a wallet or something?

Dear God, this was all too much. Still tipsy, her mind moved slower than she would've liked.

But she had to get her phone from the basement. Triage. As a trained nurse, she knew about prioritizing calamities.

To help her husband, she needed to call the police.

So she needed her phone.

So... in the dark, she had to head down the stairs into the basement.

She grit her teeth, inhaled, exhaled, summoning what nerve she had. She would treat it like entering the OR. No room for fear.

"I'll be right back," she said in a whisper towards her husband's form.

Then, double-checking the front door was still locked, she hurried forward, towards the stairs that led into the dark, dingy, unfinished basement.

She took the stairs slowly, her eyes straining in the dark. She couldn't see far...

The light from the porch, from the dipping sun didn't reach the basement stairs, and now she had to grope along the walls, moving blind.

Her fingers trailed on rough stone, then found a lacquered rail. She moved silently in the dark, into the basement, navigating based on memory alone.

Where was the basket with their phones?

She shivered, her hand finding a light switch. She flicked it on, just in case.

But the lights were still out.

Another step and she nearly twisted her ankle. She cursed, catching herself and inhaling shakily.

No time for fear.

No time for fear.

Ben needed her.

Two more quick steps and she reached the basement. The concrete was rough beneath her feet, and it took her a moment of groping in the dark to find the wall.

She moved in the dark, completely blind now. No windows down here, the electricity out, and the sun outside having dipped behind the mountains.

She was blind.

Her fingers touched something cold, and she jerked her hand back with a yelp.

"Just the pipes," she whispered to herself, straining in her alcohol-addled thoughts to remember the basement layout.

The basket with the phones had been left on the other side of the room.

She took another tottering step forward.

Then another...

Her hands splayed in front of her, searching the room.

"Where are you..." she whispered.

And then she froze.

Halfway across the room, she thought she'd heard something.

A faint giggling sound?

No... no, breathing.

Heavy breathing.

Panic flared in her, and she whirled around. But she couldn't see anything. She bit her tongue, holding back a scream.

Now she could definitely hear breathing. In, out. A footstep.

Coming closer to her.

A wave of warmth spread from her chest to her extremities, washing her with terror.

Panic flooded her system, and she held back a scream.

She had the distinct impression that whoever was down here could see her. Or at least knew where she was.

The breathing was coming closer.

Another footstep.

Something grazed her arm, and she jerked her hand back, painfully elbowing a wall behind her.

"Who's there?" she demanded, her voice shaking.

No answer.

But she could definitely hear someone moving in the dark.

The hairs on the back of her neck rose, her heart beating a million miles a minute.

Something touched her hand again, and fear burst through her chest.

Her fear turned to pure rage, and she lunged forward, knife drawn.

"Leave now!" she screamed.

She had no idea what she was doing, but she was determined to protect her husband. And clearly, whoever was down here knew where she was... How?

Could he see her?

Or maybe he could hear her breathing just like she heard him.

Everything was quiet now.

She listened, straining, her voice hoarse from the scream.

And then, a faint whisper. She could barely hear it. A voice she didn't recognize.

"Do you want him to live?"

The voice was like a mist over dark waters, barely touching down. A faint, gossamer strand of opaque sound.

"If you want him to live, do what I say..."

She swiped with her knife in the dark but struck nothing.

"Exactly what I say," the voice whispered. "Or he dies."

She let out a faint whimper, trying to reach out, to find the source of the noise.

She stumbled forward. And suddenly, her free hand struck something warm. Someone was standing directly in front of her.

And only now, unbidden but unable to be held back any longer, she loosed a desperate scream. Something grabbed her wrist.

The knife fell from her hand, clattering to the ground, and with it, any remaining hope disappeared.

Suddenly, the lights turned back on.

She went still, staring at the man in front of her, holding her wrist.

He released his grip, though.

She swallowed and stared at him, stunned. Surprise.

"O-oh... it's you. W-what?"

And then he lunged at her.

CHAPTER 1

Sweat dripped down her forehead, and Artemis gasped at the ground, her hands on her knees.

"Come on, now!" said a lazy, drawling voice from the wooden tower in the center of the warehouse. "Two more laps! How are you going to ever pass if you can't even finish the course, Checkers?"

She didn't even have the energy to glare where Cameron Forester was reclining in a chair at the top of the lookout tower as if he were some sort of lifeguard at a public swimming pool.

But this was no pool, and Artemis' exhaustion had nothing to do with swimming.

Rather, the FBI field training obstacle course had become the bane of her existence over the last three weeks.

Ever since the feds had decided not to press charges against her, contingent on her willingness to embrace more supervision under SA Grant's leadership, she'd been training ten-hour days with Forester's tutelage.

Now, standing in the dingy warehouse serving as their workout compound, Artemis felt ready to drop.

She wiped sweat from her forehead with the back of her long-sleeved shirt, a size too large for her. Her black bangs shifted from the motion across her forehead.

She leaned back and exhaled at the corrugated metal ceiling before looking back at the remainder of the obstacle course.

"Come on, Checkers! Don't slow now!" Forester called out, thumbing through a magazine. The tall, lanky ex-fighter was reclining in a sun chair he'd taken up to his lookout post, his legs crossed, his feet up on the rail.

He looked the picture of comfort as he scratched at one of his lumpy, cauliflower ears and blew a puff of air from the corner of his mouth, causing his bedraggled, auburn hair to flutter.

His dark eyes peered over the railing at her, and he flashed a thumbs up before using the same thumb to flip another page in the boxing magazine he was reading.

Artemis shook her head, returning her attention to the remainder of the obstacle course. Her hands ached from blisters, thanks to the knotted rope dangling along the climbing wall behind her.

The tire course had scuffed her shoes and shins. But by far, the most exhausting portion came in the form of the hanging bars.

Now, she faced this most hated structure of metal and wood once more, her hands already aching, her arms already strained. She glared at the thing, her jaw set.

And then she took two strides up the wooden scaffold, extended a hand, and snared the first metal bar. Her fingers nearly slipped, but she gripped tight, swinging her other arm to catch the next bar.

Her legs kicked, gaining momentum as she swung from one bar to the next.

Artemis knew it wasn't an impressive sight. Forester had told her as much, though not in so many words.

Still, she had trained her mind most of her life. As an accomplished chess master, having grown up under the tutelage of a mentalist, most of her skills had nothing to do with physical exertion.

Still, she tried to keep in shape for the sake of tournament performance.

Now, though, she could feel the strain getting to her. Three weeks of bone-tired exhaustion. Back in Seattle, she'd also faced three weeks of dreary weather with gloomy rains and thick clouds.

Three weeks of the impending field test hanging over her head. Someone impartial was going to administer the field test, and if Artemis didn't pass...

She wouldn't be able to work as a full agent under SA Grant, which meant the contingency the FBI had allowed, in order not to press charges against her and Cameron, would end in disaster.

They might even reconsider. Perhaps decide she was better placed behind prison bars.

It wasn't like she didn't have a *lot* on her mind, though.

Images flashed across her thoughts.

Helen. Her father.

Jamie leaving.

The night spent with Forester in his hotel room.

She swung from one bar to the next, and each time her hand slapped against cold metal, it was as if a new memory jogged through her brain.

Halfway across the two-dozen bars, though, she let out a yelp. Her fingers slipped. She hit the ground and scuffed her knees.

She cursed, breathing heavily.

"Nice try!" Forester called out, flashing another thumbs up.

He wasn't really paying attention though, and she didn't care anyway.

She wasn't trying to impress him.

She simply wanted to finish.

She couldn't give the feds any reason to lock her up. Too many people were counting on her. Besides...

Soon she was going to see Helen. Her brother, Tommy, had decided it would be safe enough for a rendezvous.

A family dinner. They still hadn't decided on the exact date, but Artemis could feel her excitement rising. She even gave a small, almost girlish smile. It would be just like old times.

She got to her feet, dusting off her knees and ascending the scaffolding steps again. She reached out and grabbed another bar but paused.

The thought of a Blythe family dinner was an odd one. A serial killer, a chess master, a mobster, and a man escaped from prison, all in one room.

Another flash of guilt. Pain.

Artemis tried again. This time, though, her arms gave out by the fifth monkey bar.

She fell again.

Bounced back up faster, though, and sprinted back up the scaffolding steps.

She tried again. Only halfway, this time, though.

And now, her hands were stinging.

She gasped, sweat pouring down her face once more as she reached the top step, facing the bars, and glanced down.

Both hands were pouring with blood. Blisters had popped. Some blisters, by the look of them, had formed blisters of their own.

She let out a weary sigh, dropping her head only briefly.

She could feel Forester watching her now but pushed this thought aside. Her mismatched eyes, one blue, one like wheat fields, narrowed into slits.

She wasn't going to fall again. She refused.

She swung across the bars once more.

And fell.

Again.

She tried once more.

But only made it two bars this time. The third had been slick with blood from her own hands.

"Hey, Art, maybe we can take a break!" Forester called out.

She barely even heard. She tried once more, and this time, the pain was so bad, it lanced through her right arm, sending pulses down her shoulder and along her spine.

She fell again.

She surged to her feet once more and tried again.

"Artemis!" Forester called out, a note of worry in his tone now.

She could hear him clambering down the ladder behind her.

But this only fueled her to try again. Family dinner was coming up. Her father, her sister, hell, even her brother, all needed her.

She couldn't go back behind bars.

She couldn't let them down.

"Artemis!" Forester yelled.

And suddenly she realized he was standing next to her, resting his hand on her shoulder, holding her back.

One bleeding hand was clutching the first rung. The other was hovering at her side, the fingers twisted like a talon, avoiding the bleeding blisters along her fingers and palm.

She let out a faint breath of air and glanced at Cameron, wincing sheepishly.

"You good?" said the tall, ex-fighter, frowning down at her.

He was a few inches over six foot, and so he towered above her. His brow was furrowed now, and his hand still rested on her shoulder.

She tried to push it off. "I'm fine," she said, breathing heavily.

"Yeah, well, you look like shit."

"Nice. Do you kiss your mother with that mouth?"

"Nope. But I can think of someone I'd like to."

Artemis grimaced, shifting awkwardly on her foot. She leaned back from Cameron but inwardly wanted to go the other direction.

Her eyes traced his jawline, moving down along his muscled chest. Her gaze hovered on his scarred, calloused hands, and she noticed he'd done up the buttons on his sleeves in the wrong holes.

Forester didn't suit suits.

He was a wild man at heart but also loyal. She'd never met anyone as loyal as him, nor as honest.

He just said what was on his mind without veiling it or playing any games.

Sometimes, it was alarming.

But she always knew where she stood.

"You know..." she said hesitantly, still breathing heavily from all the exercise. "I've been thinking about that night."

"Oh, what night?" Forester said innocently, picking at his fingernails.

"You know... *that* night."

He grinned. "*That* night. Couldn't forget *that* one."

She sighed, not sure if he was teasing her, or if he was just being a dick for the fun of it. This, again, was another oddity about Cameron.

More than once, he'd thrown himself into harm's way to protect her. Putting his body, his career on the line out of some projected loyalty to her that she suspected had something to do with someone else in his life.

Someone he'd once lost that she reminded him of.

The two hadn't really delved deeply into this line of reasoning.

"I... I don't..." she trailed off, sighing.

"Don't what?"

"Umm..." she bit her lip, feeling uncomfortable now, realizing she was alone in a dark warehouse with a career cage fighter.

Also, a self-declared sociopath.

And yet Forester didn't scare her in that way.

In other ways, he terrified her.

But not with her safety. She found she trusted him in a very profound way. In fact, she wasn't sure she'd ever trusted someone as much before.

"We need to talk about it," she murmured.

"About that night?"

"Yeah."

"What about it?"

She continued to bite on her lip as if the pain might jar her to her senses. In the end, though, she just shrugged. "I... I don't think it can happen again." Then, hurriedly, before he could interject, she added, "I know you want it to. And... and I do too, but it can't."

His expression was unreadable, and for Artemis—who considered herself skilled in reading non-verbal cues—that was saying something.

Forester just shrugged his massive shoulders. "How come?"

"Because it just wouldn't work."

"You said Jamie left."

"He did."

"So?"

She sighed, shaking her head, running a hand through her hair. She was sweaty, tired, and her knees were bleeding from where she'd hit the ground. Her hands were also stained red. "I'm sorry. I'm gross. Let me clean up then we can—"

"You're not," he said simply.

She blinked.

"You're not gross," he pressed. "Far as I can tell, you're a damn fine sight. Prettiest flower on these mountains." He scratched ruefully at his chin. "Flower... shit—that doesn't sound right. Wade told me that line. I take it back. Ignore the flower part. But you are damn pretty."

She gaped at him. Then felt a flush along her cheeks. "You've been talking to Wade about us?"

"Umm..." he glanced to the side then back at her. "No?"

"Why'd you phrase it like a question."

"No."

"Is that true?"

"No."

"God dammit, Forester!" She flung her arms out and began moving away, stepping over the tire obstacle course, and around the climbing wall. She even kicked at the end of the knotted rope as she passed.

"What?" he called after her, spreading his arms.

"Are you insane? I told you not to tell anyone!"

"He heard us!" Forester shouted back. Then he sighed, flung his scarred hands heavenwards, and began moving after her with his lengthy stride. He covered the distance far faster than she had.

She was moving towards the locker room in the back of the warehouse.

The space was empty, but she still wanted distance from Cameron.

Forester jogged a few steps then caught up with her. He didn't touch her, but instead said hurriedly, "We were in the same room as him, Artemis!"

"What?"

She came to a halt, whirling on him, eyes flashing.

"Damn," he said, blinking. He swallowed, staring at her, and for a moment, she almost felt as if she were the larger of the two.

He swallowed, his Adam's apple bobbing and he rubbed at his fighter's ear. "Back at the resort," he said. "In the shower." His eyes lingered on her body briefly, then he blushed and glanced up again. "Wade heard us. He wasn't sleeping *that* soundly."

She felt the flush now spreading across her entire face. She held a hand to her lips, standing stock still. "He... *heard* us?"

"Mhmm."

"Why are you saying that like it's a good thing!"

"I mean, I don't care. He's the one trying to bang that doctor friend of yours."

"The coroner? Dr. Bryant is—look, not important." She sighed, shaking her head. "It just won't work, Cameron."

He hesitated, then leaned forward, this time resting both hands on her shoulders so they faced each other. They locked eyes, and she felt the urge to push his hands away, but then the same urge turned into a desire to draw nearer.

He looked her in the eyes then said, "Tell me why, then fine. I'll drop it. Never bring it up again. Just tell me *why*."

"You... because you..." she trailed off, unsure what to say. Did she even *know* why they couldn't be together? Jamie was gone. He'd left. He'd made it clear she had to choose him or her sister, and in that choice, Jamie was the one who'd decided. Artemis couldn't turn Helen in and she wouldn't give Jamie up, so he'd chosen to leave.

But Forester...

"Because," she said simply. "You scare me."

He snorted. "That's not news, Checkers. That's history."

"Yeah, well... that night at the resort, I wasn't thinking straight."

"Sure seemed straight to me."

"My God—Cameron, is everything a quip with you?"

He grinned at her but then held up a scarred finger. "Hang on," he muttered.

A chirping noise had interrupted them. He fished his phone from his pocket, glancing at the number before answering.

Artemis was saying, "I just think maybe it'd be better if you and I can keep things professional. Is that so bad?"

A small, niggling part of her mind, though, wouldn't let it rest.

Why couldn't she see them together?

It was too soon. Jamie had left only a month before.

Too soon.

Too scary.

Too...

She grit her teeth.

"Keep it professional," she murmured again as if on auto-pilot.

It was only then she realized Cameron was nodding, speaking to the phone rather than her.

"Got it," he said. "I'll tell her."

He hung up.

She blinked. "W-what was that?"

"Didn't hear?"

"I was distracted."

He slipped his phone into his pocket, turning now and moving towards the lockers himself. "I'll drive!" he called over his shoulder.

"Drive where?" she called back, still rooted to the spot.

"Got a case," he said, glancing over his shoulder, framed in the door of the locker room.

"But... but I haven't passed the agency test yet."

"Grant says it's fine. Probationary period before the test."

"Where?"

"Couple hour drive," he said. "In the mountains. Real professional." He was chuckling to himself now and shaking his head side to side as if chagrined. "*Super* duper professional," he muttered. "You, me, a romantic getaway in the mountains. Buncha newlyweds, some wine-tasting, some late nights by the fire. Completely professional."

"What are you talking about?"

"They found a woman dead at the Cabernet Cascades."

"The vineyard?"

"Yeah. A top-three honeymoon spot in Seattle." He looked at her, gave another chuckle, then looked away, shaking his head as if he couldn't quite believe it as he walked away.

She thought she heard him giggle the word *professional* under his breath as he left.

She stood rooted to the floor.

A case at a mountain vineyard... A new case.

If Grant was asking them in on it, that meant something about the case was different.

Something that needed Artemis' *unique* perspective.

Why did they want her on *this* case? It sounded straightforward eno ugh...

But if Grant had called for her, it wouldn't be.

Artemis sighed. She tried not to let her mind conjure up all sorts of horrors as she reluctantly set off after Forester once again.

CHAPTER 2

To Artemis, the mountain scene was picturesque, ruined only slightly by the pictures of a murder victim open on the car seat next to her.

She looked away from the crime scene photos, if only to detoxify her eyes briefly, and instead stared through the windshield as Forester wound the course of winding roads into the valley.

The Cabernet Cascades Winery and Vineyard, was situated in a valley created by the cradle of two mountain passes.

A breeze carried through Forester's open window. The air was crisp, the scent of fresh pine and wood smoke enveloping the surroundings. It was an idyllic setting for the Mountain Vineyard and Winery, nestled amidst the rolling hills and lush forests.

The exterior of the winery was invitingly rustic, with its cedar shakes, black shutters, and stone accents. A large wraparound porch invited visitors to relax and take in the breathtaking views of the mountain range. A large wooden sign near the entrance announced the vineyard and winery's name.

Through the large, glass windows behind the porch railing, Artemis glimpsed the inside of the winery.

Forester pulled into a dusty parking lot facing the building, and through the glass, as they came to a stop, Artemis spotted a cozy tasting room lined with barrels of aging wines, while the walls were hung with awards and memorabilia from the winery's years in business. The tasting room was illuminated with soft lights, inviting visitors to sample the winery's signature red and white wines.

Forester flung his door open.

"Done with those?" he said, glancing at the crime scene photos.

She didn't look at them again. Didn't need to. As with most things, one look was enough for the images to be indelibly seared into her mind.

She pushed out of the car, inhaling the sweet fragrance of the vineyard's breeze.

Behind the main structure and deeper into the mountain valley, lay the winery's vineyard. Spanning acres of land, the vineyard was home to dozens of varietals of grapes, some of the area's most prized vintages. There were neat rows of vines, trained to climb up trellises and snaking their way up the side of the mountain.

Forester didn't look particularly interested in any of it. Instead, he snatched a photo from the back seat and then studied it as he slammed the front door to the car.

The two of them stood by the hood as Forester frowned at the picture.

"She was pushed then."

"That's what her husband is saying," Artemis replied.

Forester turned the file over to read the report, but then, remembering who he was with, instead of consulting the paper, he asked Artemis, "So her husband was the last one to see her?"

Artemis paused, recollecting the portion of the file she'd memorized that spoke on it, then said, "Yeah. Last one to see her. They were newlyweds. Only been in their villa about a week."

Forester scratched at his chin. "So how come we're here?" he asked.

Artemis sighed, reached back, opened the car door, and snatched a second photo from the backseat. "Because of that," she said simply.

She handed the photo to him.

He looked at it, then at her, then wrinkled his nose. "Who's this?"

"Our *second* victim," she said.

"Shit, really? Two of them?"

Artemis nodded, glancing at the gruesome photo.

She looked away again—not that it helped. "Both dead in the last two weeks. Both found under villas at the bottom of a gorge, broken on the rocks."

"And?"

"Both husbands gave the same report."

"Yeah... that someone pushed their wives?"

"No," Artemis said, her expression troubled. She heard the door to the patio open with a quiet groan. Mirroring the softness of the sound, she murmured, under her breath, "Both husbands say the same thing. That they're the ones who killed their brides."

Forester stared at her.

She shrugged.

And then turned to face a very tall, very thin man approaching on the porch to peer down a beak-like nose at the two of them.

"Hello, there!" the man called out, a smile appearing. It was a strange smile. His lips didn't part at all, revealing no teeth, and his skin pulled back like too little jam across too much biscuit. "I'm Edmond Davies," he said. "And you two must be our new guests. Andi and Kramer Givens, right?"

Artemis began to shake her head, but Forester waved and called out, "That's us, Mr. Davies. I think we spoke on the phone. How are you doing?"

Artemis noticed Forester had slipped the crime scene photos out of sight, against his leg. Then, still waving with one hand, he opened the car door with his other and pushed the photos out of sight into the vehicle, before shutting the door again.

Artemis had gone still. "Andi?" she whispered under her breath.

The tall, thin man was moving down a set of wooden stairs to join them. As he did, and as the old wood groaned, Forester whispered back. "Gotta be incognito on this one, Checkers. Laying low. You're Andi. Amateur blogger by day, bartender by night."

"And you?" she whispered as their host reached the bottom of the stairs then paused to dust something off the last step.

"I'm Kramer—super rich and hot banker. And poker player. And fighter pilot from the war."

"Which war?" she whispered fiercely.

"Not important. We got married three days ago. Try to smile." Then, now that their host had drawn near again, Forester spoke loud enough for the man to hear, beaming once more. "The place is as beautiful as the pictures," Cameron called out. "It's like nothing bad has ever happened here."

Artemis rolled her eyes. He was laying it on a little thick. Still, she supposed it could've been worse.

Mr. Davies was stuttering now, adjusting the sleeves of his suit and trying to smile at each of them in turn. "Well, well, I don't know about all of that," he said with an airy wave, clearly meant to change the subject. "But you're about an hour early. Your rooms aren't ready yet, I'm afraid."

"Room?" Forester said. "We booked one of the villas." He frowned.

Agent Desmond Wade, who was still back in the city, had been the one to book the stay. If Artemis had known they were going to masquerade as a married couple, she might have refused.

She shot a suspicious glance at Forester, wondering just how much he was enjoying her discomfort.

Mr. Davies' smile faltered for a moment before he recovered, nodding. "Ah, yes. The Givens. Givens..." He repeated the name a couple more times as he checked his phone. He didn't quite frown, but he had a lightly puzzled expression.

At last, he said, "Well... Perhaps we made a mistake on our end." He looked up now, smiling. It seemed like a genuine, warm smile, but his face only looked more stretched because of it.

The thin man said, "Currently, one of our villas is being remodeled. So I can offer you a selection of two in the valley if you'd like."

Artemis wondered if the *remodeling* had anything to do with the crime scene.

Forester nodded, his own smile returning. "Great. Can't wait to see it."

As they followed Mr. Davies through the tasting room and into the winery's back office, Artemis couldn't shake the feeling that something was off. This whole idyllic place was like something off a postcard.

As Forester provided their fake information to the guide, Artemis found herself staring out a rear-facing window.

Even when a golf cart was summoned to escort them to their temporary mountain home, she couldn't help but wonder—as they passed fields of lavender—why anyone would want to kill their bride in a place like this.

And not just *one* murder, but two in a matter of weeks. The husbands had both admitted to the crimes. But as far as she could tell, neither man had known the other.

Was it something in the wine?

Something about this place?

Her mind was still spinning as they reached their destination, left the golf cart, and Forester used the keycard to swipe them in.

The villa was stunning with a grand entrance and a view overlooking the vineyard. As they stepped inside, Forester gave a low whistle.

"Wow," he said, looking around. "This place is amazing." Inside the villa was a spacious living room, complete with plush couches and a fireplace. A large, ornate rug covered the hardwood floor, and a chandelier hung from the ceiling. Artemis couldn't help but agree with Forester—this place was truly breathtaking.

As they moved further into the villa, they discovered a fully equipped kitchen, two bedrooms, and a luxurious bathroom. Each room was decorated tastefully, with a blend of modern and rustic elements.

Forester was already unpacking his bags when Artemis sat down on the couch, still deep in thought.

"Something's not right here," she said, her eyes scanning the room.

"What do you mean?" Forester asked, glancing up from his suitcase.

"I don't know," she replied, her brow furrowing. "It's just a feeling I have. This place is too perfect. Why would someone kill their new bride in a spot like this?"

"Wedding jitters?"

"I'm being serious."

"So am I. We should talk to the husbands. They claim they did it... so I'm still not sure why Grant wants us here."

Artemis shook her head, sighing. "It was all in the report. She doesn't believe them."

"How's that?"

"Didn't you read any of it?"

"What's *reading*?"

She sighed. "Funny. Grant sees no motive. Both husbands seemed to be deeply in love. Their families report the same. They weren't caught but came forward, turning themselves in. Both within weeks of the other."

"Huh. So they admit it but under strange circumstances."

"Exactly."

Forester finally shrugged those massive shoulders of his. "So you want to poke around the villa where the last victim was killed first or speak to the husbands?"

Artemis considered this for a moment but then said, "The physical evidence will remain. But once the spouses calm down, they might change their story."

"Homicidal husbands it is then." Forester approached a small table where a laminated sign with a black arrow read, *Golf Cart Keys Here.*

He picked up the keys, tossed them once with a jangling sound, and then set out of the room.

CHAPTER 3

Artemis stood across the metal, interrogation room table, frowning at the man across from her. Benjamin Clarkson shifted nervously, swallowing as he did, resting his hands on the cold table.

She studied him, quiet, watchful.

Nothing had passed between them yet. The two of them had simply sat in silence for the last five minutes. Forester was outside the room, watching through the one-way mirror.

It had been Artemis' idea to enter the interrogation on her own. Sometimes, men found women less intimidating in an interrogation room setting.

Instead of finding this offensive, Artemis found it useful. Any tool in her belt could be used if applied properly.

Now, she studied Benjamin Clarkson.

His wife had been the most recent victim. He looked nervous, but his eyes were ringed in red as if he'd been crying.

He also looked as if he hadn't slept. His hands were tense on the table, and the cuffs occasionally rattled, suggesting his hands were trembling.

Artemis decided the best route forward was to approach it carefully, with caution.

She adopted a gentle tone. As she did, she thought through the communication training she'd been assigned. She'd already memorized the manual, but the practical side of it was still fresh.

Normally, Forester wouldn't have wanted her alone in a room with a suspect, but both of them knew that if she was supposed to pass the FBI competency test, she'd have to find her way.

Besides, Benjamin looked like a frat boy who'd gone for a weekend of golfing. Hardly the most physically threatening specimen.

Now, though, she cleared her throat and, in a soft voice said. "My name is Artemis Blythe. And you are?"

He blinked, as if slapped. The sound in the room seemed to have taken him off guard. He just shook his head and shrugged.

She nodded.

Artemis leaned forward, resting her arms on the table. "Benjamin, can you tell me about your relationship with your wife?"

Benjamin's eyes darted around the room, avoiding hers. "We were happy. We loved each other. I don't know what happened." He spoke in quick, stilted language, cutting each sentence short.

His eyes were still ringed red, and his voice quavered with emotion. An act?

He'd confessed to the murder already.

But now, sitting across from him, Artemis couldn't help but agree with Special Agent Grant.

Something was off.

It was up to her to find out what, though.

She didn't allow these thoughts to reveal themselves across her countenance, however. Her tone still calm, Artemis nodded, then continued, "I understand. But can you think of any reason why someone would want to harm her?"

Benjamin shook his head, "Someone?"

"Yes. Someone."

"I... I did it. I already told you."

She glanced briefly towards the one-way mirror. She couldn't see Forester, but he could see them.

"So you're sticking to that story, then?"

He let out a faint sigh and dropped his head, holding it in his hands. Hair that was a few inches long pressed between his fingers in a forlorn way.

"It's the truth," he whispered.

Artemis nodded, still watching him, cataloging everything she saw.

"You seem upset."

"My wife's dead," he replied. "I... I loved her." He almost moaned this last part.

"So why did you kill her?"

"What?" he looked up.

"You said you killed her."

"Right. Oh... Yeah... yeah, I did." He blinked a couple of times now, looking briefly confused.

Artemis hesitated, then tried another approach. "Besides *you*... can you think of anyone who'd want to harm her?"

"Anyone else? No, I can't. She was loved by everyone. She didn't have any enemies."

Artemis leaned back in her chair, studying him for a moment. "Benjamin, I need you to be completely honest with me. Is there anything you're holding back?"

Benjamin's eyes widened, "No, I swear. I've told you everything. I killed her. She was the love of my life. My best friend... and I... I killed her."

Again, his voice shook with emotion. His eyes were wide. He looked as if he were barely holding it together, and whenever he spoke, he looked stunned at his own words.

She hesitated, then said, "Why don't you tell me what happened yesterday? Walk me through it."

"Do I have to?"

"Please, I'm just trying to understand."

He sighed, blowing his long bangs with a puff of air. Then, in a slow voice, he said, "We arrived here two days ago." A ghost of a smile. "It was our honeymoon."

"I heard," Artemis continued in that gentle voice. "Did anything happen? Did you two get into a fight?"

"No. No, I was making her dinner."

"Dinner. That was before you say you killed her."

"I don't just *say* it. I did."

"Okay."

"You have to believe me!"

Artemis frowned. She hesitated, then said, "Why is it so important that I believe you killed your wife?"

"Because I did it!"

"You did?"

"Yes!"

She crossed her arms. "Do you see why it's strange, Mr. Clarkson, for someone to be so adamant they murdered their wife?"

"I... what?"

Artemis leaned forward again, changing her posture, she rested her hands flat on the table, staring right at him. "Do you know Leo Ramirez?"

"Wh-who?"

"Mr. Ramirez' wife was killed a couple weeks before. He claimed he did it as well. Do you know him?"

"N-no... Oh, God, how horrible."

"It is horrible, isn't it? Did you and your wife have some sort of falling out? Some disagreement? Was it a crime of passion?"

"No..." He shook his head, pale. "God... I can't believe she's gone." His voice trembled now as he said it.

Artemis sat back in her chair, studying Benjamin. There was something off about him, she just couldn't put her finger on it. She decided to take a different approach, to see if she could catch him off guard.

"Benjamin, may I ask you a personal question?"

He looked up at her, his eyes full of sadness. "Sure."

"Have you ever hired a prostitute?"

Benjamin's eyes widened in shock. "What? No, I haven't. Why are you asking me that?"

"Just a hunch," Artemis said with a shrug. "Sometimes, men who feel trapped in their relationships seek out other women."

"I loved my wife," Benjamin said, his voice rising in defense. "I would never cheat on her."

"I see," Artemis said, making a note in her pad. It was really just a scribble, nothing substantial.

All of it was to see his reaction. His voice had risen an octave at the question. He'd looked embarrassed, angry even.

The idea he would cheat on his wife was offensive to him.

She hadn't *actually* thought he'd been with a prostitute. It could've been any question, really, to get him emotionally engaged.

But the point was that when people were angry, they said more.

By asking about faithfulness, she'd seen who he was.

45

A faithful man. Loyal. Offended, even, by the thought of infidelity.

So why the hell had he killed his wife?

"Tell me exactly what happened that night. After dinner."

"We never got dinner. Hang on, did someone say I was seeing a prostitute?"

"Were you?"

"No! Absolutely not. Never! I would never cheat on her."

"Because you loved her."

"Exactly."

"So why did you kill her?"

"What?"

"*Why* did you kill her?"

He blinked a couple of times as if he couldn't quite understand the question. Then, he frowned, paused, then said, "I need to speak with my lawyer."

Artemis met his gaze, trying to read his expression. He felt like a shell... like a mimic. Some sort of puppet.

It didn't feel like she was having a conversation with the real Benjamin Clarkson.

He looked confused...

"Did they run any blood tests on you, Benjamin?"

"Yeah. Yeah, I think so."

She nodded, then said, "I'll be right back."

She pushed to her feet, then, she turned to the door, pushing out into the hall, a troubled look on her face.

Something was definitely off.

He was acting strangely... But if they'd done a blood test, then she'd be able to see if he'd been drugged.

She shook her head, allowing the door to close behind her as she stood in the dingy hallway, turning to face Cameron.

"Weird, right?" he said, looking at her.

"Very weird," she replied. "I want to see that bloodwork."

CHAPTER 4

Her impatience grew, waiting for Forester to return with the blood-work. Artemis paced in the breakroom, scowling at the vending machine where a bag of dried apple slices in a blue, plastic wrapping had gotten stuck.

Through the large window off to the right, affected only slightly by the dark, privacy tint, she gazed at the base of the mountains. A half-hour, winding drive from the vineyard and honeymoon spot, the small police precinct didn't even seem to have air conditioning.

She shook her head, glancing away from the window.

Movement by the glass window overlooking the hall caught her attention, though, and she turned sharply to watch as Agent Forester approached.

He was frowning hesitantly, glancing at a printed sheet of paper as he drew near.

He pushed open the door, and gave a quick shake of his head, running a hand through his messy, brown hair.

"What's wrong?" she said instantly.

"No dice."

"Where's the bloodwork?"

"Someone put a hold on it. One of the people at the lab."

"I... don't understand. Why?" Artemis asked, frowning.

Forester shrugged, wincing and scratching at his chin. He let out a sigh and turned the paper so she could see.

"It says here that the bloodwork has been flagged due to possible contamination," he explained.

Artemis stared at the sheet of paper, her heart sinking. This was not good news.

"What does that mean?" she asked, feeling a sense of unease.

"It means they can't verify if the results are accurate. They want to run the tests again."

"But that will take time," Artemis said, feeling frustration building inside her. Time was something they didn't have. They needed answers now.

"I know," Forester replied, looking equally frustrated. "I'll call the lab and see if we can expedite the process. But in the meantime, we'll have to work with what we have."

Artemis nodded, trying to push aside her disappointment. She knew she had to keep pushing forward, even without the bloodwork.

"Alright," she said, clenching her fists. "Let's go back and talk to Clarkson. Maybe we can find something else."

"We still need to check out the crime scene," he reminded her. He quirked an eyebrow, watching her.

She frowned. "What?"

"What do you mean, *what*?"

"You're giving me that look... Did I miss something? This isn't a field exercise, Cameron. You can't expect me to remember protocol."

"Well, the test proctors are sure going to expect it. We still need to secure the crime scene. That's pretty damn important, wouldn't you say?"

She huffed, snatching the piece of paper from his hand, staring at it, and then going still. "Hang on," she murmured.

"What?"

"The person who put a hold on the results."

"What about them?"

"Look at the name!" Artemis said, her curiosity now mounting. She turned the paper so Forester could see.

He leaned in, wrinkling his nose in confusion. The two of them studied the paper, and then Forester blinked.

"Dr. Bryant?"

"Miracle was running the bloodwork?" Artemis asked quietly. "Huh... It isn't like Bryant to have to run something twice."

"Even flamboyant geniuses make mistakes," Forester shot back.

"Yeah... Yeah, I guess so." Artemis brushed back her dark bangs and began to turn towards the door.

But suddenly, she paused, still gripping the sheet of paper.

"What is it?" Forester said, reading her expression.

"I guess we're not going to have to wait to find out," Artemis murmured.

"What? Why not?"

"Because. Look. She's here."

"Who is... oh, shit. What..."

Forester and Artemis were now both staring through the tinted window facing the parking lot.

A woman was marching towards the precinct door. She was also staring at the window, though, there shouldn't have been any way for her to see either of the agents. Regardless, she was staring through the dark glass as if she could look right at them.

As she walked, there was something lithe and graceful about the middle-aged, black woman's movements. Her hair was now shaved on one side, and the rest tied back in a pink pony-tail with bright, glittering highlights. She wore extra-long eyelashes, which fluttered, and purple eyeshadow. A bright, white shirt had a stencil of a glittering star, and the phrase *You can reach the sun!*

Dr. Bryant, the coroner from back in Pinelake, often worked with the FBI. She was one of the few people who'd trusted Artemis before evidence had come through to clear Artemis' name.

Now, though, Dr. Bryant's usual beaming smile and energetically optimistic personality had been replaced by a scowl and a strict march.

She moved towards the precinct doors, and after a moment, Artemis and Forester watched through the window in the wall, along the hall, as the woman passed through security, retrieved her keys and pink wallet from a gray, plastic tupperware, and then marched down the hall in their direction.

She paused only briefly, scanning the room once before her eyes landed on Forester and Artemis.

Her purple eye shadow stretched as her eyes widened. She took a long breath, the glitter on her sparkling shirt rising on her ample bosom once. She combed back her bright, pink hair, making sure no strands were free from the green scrunchie.

And then, with an air of dignity and determination, she strode down the hall, pushed open the door, and confronted the two agents with a severe glare.

"You two are on my baby brother's case?"

Artemis blinked in surprise.

"Hey there, doc," Forester said.

Miracle, unable to forget her usual cheerful self, took a second to flash a smile at Cameron followed by a quick nod and a thumbs up. But then she repeated, a bit more firmly, "Are you two investigating Benjamin's case?"

Artemis blinked in surprise. "Benjamin... *Clarkson*?" she said.

Dr. Bryant nodded once, hooked the door behind her, and swept it shut, causing sequins along her shoes to flash under a home-stitched pant leg.

Then, the bedazzling woman turned once more, crossing her arms. "Clarkson, yes. He took his wife's last name when they were married. H e *was* Benjamin Bryant. Didn't like the alliteration. I'm here to tell you he didn't do it."

Her chin was high, her eyes holding something like a thunderstorm beneath the dark, fluttering, mascara-streaked lashes.

Before either of them could reply, the normally effusive woman continued, waving a hand about now like a conductor's wand. Long, curling, paste-on fingernails flashed back and forth, displaying gloss and small paintings on each nail.

Dr. Bryant was exclaiming, "He couldn't have! He loved Gina!" She wagged a finger directly at Cameron now. "Oooh, you big galoot! Just like you to throw a poor, innocent, little babe behind bars. Just wait until I get my hands on you, Cameron Fitzgerald!"

"Umm... My last name's not Fitz—"

"Did I *say* I was finished! My baby brother loses his angel of a wife, and you drag him through the mud over it! And *this* is how I learn!" she was still gesticulating wildly.

Her chest swelled again, and for a moment, Artemis half expected the roar of a lioness to resonate from the woman's lips.

Artemis tried twice more to get a word in edgewise, but Miracle had built up a head of steam, clearly having rehearsed some of the diatribe on her drive over.

"Of course I had to put a hold on it! My brother didn't hurt anyone! He couldn't. I once saw him cry for stepping on a fly! God's honest truth—Jesus as my witness!" she said, making a crossing motion over her chest, which caused one of her paste-on fingernails to catch on her white sweater.

She paused, trying to disentangle from a sparkling sequin.

Artemis took this chance to cut in. "He admitted to doing it, Dr. Bryant. He said he killed her. He still does."

The moment Artemis finished, Dr. Bryant blinked once. Her fingernail was still stuck on a strand of her sweater, but she seemed to forget it, briefly, her hand just dangling in the air.

She blinked once, owlishly.

"E-excuse me?" she said, clearing her throat daintily. "I... I think I misheard you."

Artemis winced apologetically, took a step forward, and reached out a comforting hand, placing it on the woman's shoulder. Now that Artemis drew near, she smelled the bright, flowery fragrance of a strong perfume. The scent reminded Artemis of tulips and rainforests.

She met Dr. Bryant's gaze, leaving her hand on the woman's shoulder, and said, "He admitted it. Just now. He did in the initial report as well."

"That's not possible," Dr. Bryant said, bristling.

"It's true."

She hesitated, staring at Cameron now, back at Artemis, then at Cameron once more.

"It's not possible," she repeated, her voice trembling. "My brother could never hurt anyone, especially not Gina. They were soulmates."

Artemis could see the pain etched on Dr. Bryant's face, and she knew it was going to be a difficult conversation.

"Dr. Bryant, I understand this is hard for you to hear, but we have evidence. Benjamin confessed to the murder," Artemis explained gently.

Dr. Bryant's eyes widened in disbelief. "But... but that's impossible." She looked scared now, panicked. She hesitated, then said, quickly. "He was with me that night. We were watching a movie together!"

Artemis and Forester exchanged a glance. "He came to visit his sister... on his honeymoon?" Artemis said gently, her hand still touching the woman's arm.

Dr. Bryant paused, winced, but then doubled down. "Yes. Yes, whatever he's saying, it can't be true. He was with me. He never hurt her."

"What movie?" Forester asked.

"Excuse me?"

"You said you two were watching a movie. What was it?"

Dr. Bryant hesitated for a moment before answering. "It was... 'The Notebook.' Gina's favorite," she added, her voice cracking with emotion.

Artemis felt a pang of sympathy for Dr. Bryant. Losing a loved one was never easy, and learning that they had been killed by someone close to them would only make things worse.

"Dr. Bryant," Artemis said quietly, "If we check the cameras outside your lab, will we see you there until late at night? Or will we see you leave and go see your brother?"

Dr. Bryant bit her lip now, and tears were welling in the woman's eyes. She opened her mouth, closed it again.

And then she collapsed on the small, lumpy couch facing the vending machine.

She hunched over, holding her head in her hands and rocking back and forth. "Oh, Lord Jesus, give me strength!" she exclaimed.

Artemis sighed softly, glancing at Forester.

He winced, shrugged, and pointed at Artemis. Then he pointed at himself and the door.

Then, before she could protest, Cameron beat a hasty retreat, still clutching the paper printout which made a fluttering sound as he tried to escape the room with the sobbing woman.

Dr. Bryant's mascara was streaking now. "A-Artemis," she said, gasping. "Artemis..."

"Yes, Miracle?" Artemis leaned in now, feeling her sympathy rising even more. She wanted to reach out and hug the woman.

She knew what it was to have a sibling in danger.

Hell... she knew better than most what it was to have a sibling accused of murder.

Dr. Bryant hiccupped then looked up, her eyes brimming, her face streaked. She said, in a shaky voice, "I'm... I'm sorry I lied."

"Lied about what?" Artemis replied gently.

"He wasn't with me. He wasn't. I haven't seen him in a week, but... but he couldn't have done this."

She cleared her throat and straightened suddenly, a desperation in her eyes. "Let me speak with him. Can I do that? I'll make him see sense. Yes," she said, nodding firmly and launching spryly back to her feet. "Yes, that settles it. I'll speak to him. He'll see sense. He'll tell me the truth."

Artemis wanted to protest. She knew that it wasn't even *close* to protocol to let Dr. Bryant in the interrogation room...

Miracle's eyes flashed once more though as she read Artemis' expression. Then, in a low voice, she murmured, "I know it isn't like a Christian woman to hold a favor over someone's head..." She paused, but then said, even more firmly, "But I remember someone else in dire straits who came to visit me. Someone who asked me to trust them."

Artemis sighed.

She could remember the instance all too well.

"I... I don't know," Artemis whispered. "I don't know if you *want* to see him like this, Miracle. Not now."

But the older woman was shaking her head hurriedly. "Please, Artemis. *Please.* He's my baby brother. The only family I have left. *Please!*"

Artemis paused, winced, but then both of their attention was caught by someone in the doorway.

A cleared throat.

A panicked widening of the eyes from the man standing there.

Forester was holding the door open but was also gripping the arm of Benjamin Clarkson.

Clarkson's hands were cuffed behind his back, but he was standing in the doorway where Forester had evidently brought him, staring directly at his older sister.

Benjamin gaped for a moment like a wounded trout. Then, in a whisper, he said, "Miracle, you shouldn't have come here."

"Benny!" she exclaimed, hurrying forward now.

Forester held out a halting hand, though. "Don't touch the suspect, please."

Miracle stopped as if she'd been slapped, just as much at the hand gesture as at the word *suspect*.

She stared at her little brother a moment longer, swallowing as she did.

Then, she whispered, "Benny... they're saying the most horrible things. They're saying..."

"I killed her," he cut in before she could finish.

"Exactly! How awful!"

"No... No, I'm telling you," he said, his voice dull. "I did it. I killed her. I'm so, so sorry."

His eyes welled up as he held his sister's gaze. The two of them locked eyes, frozen in place.

"It's a lie," Miracle whispered.

"No," he said gently. "It isn't. I killed my wife. I killed Gina."

CHAPTER 5

Artemis cautiously approached Dr. Bryant where she sat hunched on a bench under a tall western larch, the branches spread like a fan above her.

Dr. Bryant was breathing quickly, pausing every now and then to dab at her eyes with her sleeve.

"Miracle," Artemis said gently, pausing under the shadow of the fir tree, the pine needles crunching underfoot.

The precinct, fifty paces behind them, stood sentry, the large windows unblinking, like the glare of an owl, watching the two women.

Dr. Bryant sniffed and looked up with red-ringed eyes. The same eyes as Benjamin.

"Artemis," Dr. Bryant said hesitantly, and there was a faint tremor to her voice. For a brief moment, the middle-aged coroner looked like a child lost in the woods, pleading for help.

Artemis felt a pang in her heart.

Dr. Bryant tried to smile, but her heart wasn't in it, and so in the end, she looked down at the ground again, twisting her hands in her lap.

"I... I'm sorry," Miracle whispered quietly. "I didn't mean to cause trouble. I came in... guns-blazing..." She hesitated, glanced at the precinct, cleared her throat, and quickly added, "Metaphorically. I didn't mean to be rude. I just..." Her shoulders trembled, and she didn't look up. "He's the only family I have left," she repeated the refrain from earlier. "I just... I can't believe he would do that... *Why* would he do that?"

Her hands continued to twist, but something was gone in her posture. A spark, a vitality that so often appeared in her movements. Artemis had often likened Dr. Bryant's motions to those of a dancer.

Now, though, the coroner just looked sad and exhausted.

Artemis sat down next to Dr. Bryant, careful not to startle her. She placed a hand on the coroner's shaking shoulder, trying to offer some comfort. "It's okay, Miracle. You don't have to apologize. I understand how much Benjamin means to you," she said softly. "My own brother ... and my..." Artemis paused. She'd been about to say *sister* but caught herself.

Helen was still being watched closely. Artemis still couldn't see her sister.

Not until the FBI training was over, until the surveillance keeping an eye on her was lax once more.

She couldn't afford to lead them to her sister. To her father.

She sat quietly, frowning, feeling the same hurt Bryant felt resonate through her own body.

Dr. Bryant took a deep breath and wiped her eyes with the back of her hand. "I just can't help but think that I missed something. That I should have seen the signs or done something to prevent this," she said, her voice trembling with emotion. "He was such a sweetheart growing up. Not a violent bone in his body. I once saw him stop his car just to help a pack of geese across a highway. He did that sort of thing all the time. I should've seen something. Should've helped!" Her voice tremored even more violently, her hands following suit.

Artemis shook her head. "You can't blame yourself, Miracle. Sometimes people do things that we can't predict or explain. All we can do is be there for each other and try to make sense of it all."

Dr. Bryant nodded slowly, her hands still fidgeting in her lap. "I just feel so lost right now. Like everything I thought I knew has been turned upside down."

Artemis squeezed her shoulder gently. "I know. It's a lot to take in. But we'll get through this together. And who knows, maybe we'll even find a way to help Benjamin."

Dr. Bryant looked up at her, her eyes shining with hope. "Do you really think so?"

Artemis hesitated. She hadn't really *meant* it that way. She'd hoped her words would simply be consolatory.

But then, she hesitated...

"He... he was acting strangely when we spoke to him," Artemis said quietly. "He seemed off. That's why I wanted the bloodwork. To see if maybe he was drugged."

But Dr. Bryant was shaking her head. The woman got to her feet now, pacing in front of the bench, pine needles crunching, her features cast in the shadow of the fir tree branches.

She said, "I ran the bloodwork. Nothing. Completely clean."

Artemis frowned. "What about the wound on his head. It's a small cut, but he was struck."

Dr. Bryant shook her head. "I saw that. A contusion. Self-inflicted."

"Really? Self?"

"Yes. He did it to himself. The angle was wrong for anyone else to have done it." Now, Dr. Bryant was speaking more matter-of-factly, like the professional she was.

Artemis, though, stood up as well, frowning. She could feel a cold chill moving along her spine. "You're sure he hit himself?"

"Very. His nose would've impeded a blow from someone else. He would've intentionally had to turn his face upwards, pause and hold the motion. Plus my brother is right-handed, so for it to be someone else, they would've had to be left-handed. The odds of that are significantly lower. Most likely, he hit himself." Dr. Bryant shrugged. "I assumed he was punishing himself for what he did." Her voice held firm now, her eyes fierce. Now that they were speaking about work, she seemed able to distract herself a bit.

But Artemis was shaking her head, turning now to frown back in the direction of the precinct.

"What's the matter?" Miracle asked.

"If he hit himself..." Artemis paused, hesitant. It wasn't adding up. None of it did. She said, "We need to go see that villa."

"Excuse me?"

Artemis turned to look Bryant in the eye. "The villa where your brother was staying. That's where... where Gina died. She was found at the bottom of the bluff, but her body was posed."

"Posed how?"

"As if she were sleeping," Artemis said quietly, "Hands tucked under her head. Someone pushed her, then posed her."

"Someone... Not Benjamin?"

"Well... Grant was the one who sent us. She seems to think there's more here than meets the eye." Now that Artemis thought about it, she supposed that Grant's connection to Miracle Bryant had been the reason the supervising agent had looked into the case.

One thing could be said for Agent Grant. She was loyal to her subordinates.

She went out of her way to protect her nephew. She'd gone to bat to keep Artemis out of jail.

And now?

Now, it seemed obvious, she was hoping to clear the name of the coroner's brother.

Artemis felt her fondness for Grant growing, if only a little. But thinking too much about the supervising agent made her also think of the upcoming FBI test.

She pushed the thought from her mind with a shiver. She hesitated, then said, "Forester is still conducting the interrogation. I could use a fresh set of eyes." Artemis knew it was completely abnormal to invite the sister of a suspect to a crime scene.

But Dr. Bryant had been there for her as well.

Artemis could still remember the encounter in the nursing home, where Miracle had decided to trust Artemis.

Cops had been knocking on the door, looking for her, but Dr. Bryant hadn't turned Artemis in.

If that didn't buy some good will, nothing would.

Artemis nodded firmly, more to convince herself than Dr. Bryant, and said, "Let's go. We can take your car."

Artemis didn't need to scan the parking lot to guess which vehicle belonged to Miracle.

Only one, small, bright pink, electric vehicle had been parked between the faded white lines. Through the windshield, Artemis spotted a dream catcher dangling from the rearview mirror, and a bible verse sticker on the rear windshield which read, *John 17:18-23*. Below it, was the swooping word *Love* in cursive handwriting.

Dr. Bryant was wiping her eyes again but sniffed, summoned her resolve, and moved hastily towards the parked car.

"Where's the villa then?" Miracle said, shooting Artemis a quick glance as the two women reached the vehicle.

"I'll direct you," Artemis said quietly. "I... I can't promise anything, Miracle. But it's at least worth looking into. Still..." Artemis paused, hand on the top of the pink vehicle. "Your brother admitted to the crime. He struck himself, according to your professional opinion. There was nothing in his blood... And in cases like these, we often look at the spouse first."

She shrugged, trying to look equally apologetic and sincere.

But Miracle was no longer listening. Instead, she'd opened the front door, slid into the driver's seat, and drummed her fingers against the steering wheel in the dreaded anticipation of visiting her sister-in-law's murder scene.

CHAPTER 6

Noah Fieldgreen yelped in surprise as his wife nearly tumbled over the ridge. He lunged, trying to grab her sleeve.

But she laughed and pushed off the railing, showing that she'd been gripping it all the time.

"I'm fine, silly," Cynthia said, aiming her dazzling smile back at her new husband.

Noah swallowed, breathing quickly but covering with a quick smile. "Don't scare me like that!" he exclaimed.

The two of them found themselves on a mountain trail in the Cascades, both hiking up to one of their favorite lookout spots.

They'd been married in these mountains only two weeks before, and the two of them loved the outdoors. Hiking was one of Noah's favorite pastimes.

Hiking with Cynthia, though?

Sheer bliss.

He leaned in, giving her a quick peck on the cheek. Then, he wrapped an arm around her waist and guided her onto his other side, away from the ledge. "You stay right there," he said, chuckling.

She rolled her eyes, long lashes fluttering, but then leaned in and gave him a proper kiss.

For a moment, everything else disappeared. The two of them stood on the winding hiking trail, under a sheer bluff dappled with gray and beige stone. They overlooked the rail, surrounded by trees and mountains as far as the eye could see. In the distance was the sound of rushing water from the waterfall they'd been venturing to see.

But now, not even the scenery could distract Noah from the lips of his high-school sweetheart. For ten years they'd dated. He'd finally mustered the courage to pop the question...

She breathed heavily, pushing her fingers against his chest and looking up at him. Her smile had diminished briefly, though. She was staring past him, towards the bluff.

He hesitated, briefly wondering if he'd done something wrong. But then he realized the look of fear in her gaze had nothing to do with him.

He turned as well, peering up at the cliff.

He spotted it.

A wolf.

It was staring down at them. The beast was panting, its tongue hanging out.

"Crap," Noah whispered.

"Don't move," Cynthia replied in a whisper. "I read that they only chase moving things."

"Is that true?"

"Umm... maybe not. I don't know. But just stay still. It's only one."

For a moment, the two lovers, arm in arm, stared up at the toothy creature.

The wolf cocked its shaggy head, ears twitching as it stared down its long, grizzled muzzle at them.

"Shoo!" Noah said at last.

The wolf gave him a baleful look with yellow eyes, then turned and scampered off into the trees.

Noah gave a little relieved laugh. He shook his head, massaging at his eyes.

"That was a close one," he muttered.

And that's when he was pushed.

Hard, shoved from behind.

He stumbled, hit the rail with the back of his leg. His knees buckled.

He'd been in the middle of exhaling, so he didn't even have the breath to scream out.

It happened so suddenly.

He tumbled back. Air catching him. Then wind around him. His clothing ruffling.

A scream, never to be released, caught in his lungs as he tumbled to his death.

The final image before his soul fled was that of a single figure standing by the railing, staring down at his plummeting form.

CHAPTER 7

The yellow crime scene tape created a bright X across the front door of the ornate trim circling the villa's door.

Artemis stepped up the solid, varnished, wooden steps onto a quaint porch under a buttressing wooden terrace.

She shivered as a breeze came whistling through, carried over the open canyon to their back, unobstructed by trees.

Dr. Bryant was bustling up the stairs as well, breathing somewhat heavily from the effort of hiking the sheer driveway, leaving their car on the side of the road.

Artemis waited for Bryant to join her, and as she did, she looked out at the mountain pass below.

The sharp drop over the edge of the cliff had been the murder weapon of choice.

Benjamin had claimed full culpability.

His wife had broken on the rocks far below.

Artemis peered carefully through the slats in the wooden railing, staring down at the sharp, jagged rocks extending towards her.

Dr. Bryant was huffing and puffing now as she joined Artemis on the porch. She had a new light in her eyes, though, and was now marching towards the crime scene tape.

"Check the doors and windows for a break-in!" Bryant was saying hurriedly. "If someone broke in, then it couldn't have been my brother's fault."

Artemis nodded faintly, still staring out at the scenic view of the mountain pass. A sheer drop to the valley below, jagged rocks instead of grass and dirt and trees, a landscape of sheer rigidity.

Artemis turned away from the railing, taking a deep breath to steady herself. As she stepped towards the villa's front door, she couldn't help but feel her mind turning wishful.

Hopeful they'd discover something that might counteract Benjamin's story. Something that might give Dr. Bryant some hope.

Artemis pushed open the door, wincing at the sound of the creaky hinges. The villa was dark, the only light coming from the sun filtering in through the windows. They made their way through the living room, careful not to disturb anything. Artemis could see that Dr.

Bryant was nervous, her hands shaking slightly as she searched for any signs of a break-in.

Artemis walked over to the windows and began examining them one by one. The glass was intact, but there were bloodstains by the front door.

She paused, frowning.

Dr. Bryant, who'd regained her breath, was peering down at the blood, her expression quizzical.

For a brief moment, the woman looked the same way Artemis so often did when studying a chess puzzle.

Now, Bryant frowned, her eyes moving to a discarded branch that had been hidden behind the door jamb.

Artemis approached, frowning. "You say your brother struck himself, right?"

"Yeah."

"Must've hit himself pretty hard..."

"Yes... He lay on the ground here," Bryant said quietly. Her fabulously adorned fingernails waved in the air above the bloodstain as if she were casting a spell. "Lateral hairs are pressed into the blood."

Artemis frowned, glancing at the coroner. "What does that mean?"

"It means that he hit himself... then either faked a lack of consciousness... or really was unconscious."

"Why would he fake being unconscious?"

She shook her head, biting her lip. Artemis could tell how hard Bryant was trying to keep it all together.

Artemis dropped to her haunches now, staring at the stain on the floor, the club by the door.

A strangely positioned club. Why by the front door? Artemis' expression twisted into a frown. "It's a strange place to hit yourself, yeah?"

"He did. I guarantee it."

"You're that certain?"

Dr. Bryant just nodded a single time, her head bobbing. "I know this language, dear." There was a soft sadness to her voice.

Artemis pushed back to her feet now, still frowning. "He struck himself then went unconscious. Why? If he was planning on killing his wife, why attack *himself*? A mental break?"

"Did he look mentally broken?"

Artemis shook her head, biting her lower lip now. "No... No, it just doesn't make sense."

She paused, sighed, then turned to move towards the balcony. "That's where she was pushed," Artemis said, pointing towards the cracked railing visible through the glass. The crime scene photographers had made sure to take many pictures of the splintered wooden rail.

Now, as Artemis drew closer, she tried to piece together what was evident.

No splinters on the ground. No sign of a struggle—all the furniture on the terrace was perfectly arranged.

Gina had either been overpowered or taken by surprise. Artemis looked along the rail, standing on the porch now, a rising breeze fluffing her dark hair.

She couldn't help but feel a sense of unease. It was too quiet, too still. There were no birds chirping or leaves rustling. It was as though the world had come to a standstill in the wake of the tragedy.

Artemis leaned over the railing, staring down at the jagged rocks. She could feel the wind tugging at her clothes, threatening to pull her over the edge. A shiver raced down her spine, and she stepped back, her heart pounding. What could possibly drive someone to kill the love of their life in cold blood?

And in such a horrible way?

She pictured the plummet, the brief moment before a scream erupted from the victim's lips.

Dr. Bryant joined her on the balcony, her expression grim. "This is where he says he did it, then?" she said softly. "This is where my sister-in-law died."

Artemis nodded faintly, her eyes scanning the area for any clues. And then she saw it—a glint of metal on the ground. She leaned down and picked it up, her eyes widening.

It was a ring. A diamond ring.

She turned to Dr. Bryant, holding out the ring and glancing at the many jeweled circlets around the woman's fingers. "This isn't yours, is it?"

Bryant shook her head, her eyes widening. "No... That's not mine. I recognize it, though. It's Gina's engagement ring."

Artemis frowned. "She took her ring off?"

"Or someone else did."

"Then just left it here," Artemis said quietly. She stared at the ring, then slipped it into her pocket. "Had Benjamin removed the ring before killing his wife out of a sense of guilt?"

She shivered, shaking her head and turning away from the railing. "We should check the rest of the house," she murmured.

As they turned back towards the doors, though, Artemis' phone suddenly began to ring.

She held up a finger, as if to say *one moment,* then answered. "Forester?"

"Hey, Checkers. Leo Ramirez is here."

"Right now? I thought he wasn't due from county for another hour."

"They had a spare set of boots. He's settling. No lawyer, either."

Artemis frowned, phone grazing her cheek. "How... how does he look?"

A pause, a cleared throat. Forester said, "I mean, you know how I am with emotions."

"Right. Try your best."

"He looks... sad? Hungry. One of the two, maybe both. Hey, have you had lunch yet?"

"Are you asking me out to lunch?"

"Well?"

She sighed. "I'll be there soon. Don't speak to him without me."

Forester gave a whistle.

"What?"

"Nothing. I just like it when you get all bossy-pants."

She winced, feeling her cheeks flush. "Sorry. I wasn't trying to tell you what to do."

"No. I'm serious. I like it." He laughed. "See you in a jiff."

He hung up.

She sighed, stared at the phone, then looked back at Dr. Bryant. "Gonna check downstairs real quick, then we gotta go. Our second would-be murderer just showed up."

CHAPTER 8

Back in the interrogation room, Artemis wasn't sure what she'd been expecting, but it hadn't been *this*. The man was sleeping on the table, his head resting on his hands.

Leo Ramirez, widower and confessed murderer of the late Sasha Ramirez, looked like a swaddled babe settled down for a nap.

She stared across the cold room. This time, Forester was already at the table, waiting for her. His hands were crossed behind his head and his legs thrown up, resting on the metal table.

He glanced back as she allowed the door to the cold, dark room to shut behind her. Then gave her a cheeky nod.

"He's been zonked out for the last ten minutes. Guessing he hasn't had much sleep."

Artemis slowly approached, fiddling with the wedding ring in her pocket. She'd checked with the photographs from the Ramirez crime scene as well.

Her wedding ring had *also* been removed.

Strange. Two men, so disconnected, somehow so similar all the same.

"Did you know Benjamin Clarkson?" she said quietly from the corner of the room.

No response.

Forester glanced at the apparently slumbering man.

But Artemis said, "I know you're not sleeping."

He didn't react, but she could already see through the attempted deception. His eyes were far *too* still, and his breathing changed pattern when she'd entered the room.

She just said, in an even tone, "I asked if you knew Benjamin Clarkson."

Leo Ramirez hesitated a moment longer, and then he continued the farce by fluttering his eyes, glancing at her, and pretending as if he were confused.

"Er, sorry... hello. Who are you?"

He spoke with a faint accent. Leo looked like he was in his late thirties, with dark hair and dark eyes that were currently pretending to be drowsy.

Artemis raised an eyebrow, unimpressed. "Cut the act, Mr. Ramirez."

Leo sighed, finally sitting up and rubbing his face tiredly. "I don't know any Benjamin Clarkson."

Artemis leaned forward, folding her arms on the table.

She pulled out the diamond ring, sliding it across the table towards him. "Do you recognize this?"

Leo just wrinkled his nose. "No... should I?"

"That's what we're trying to figure out," Artemis said slowly. She tapped a finger against her lips. So far, he didn't look as if he were being deceptive.

His eyes were drooping though, once more, and he looked uncomfortable.

She said, "And what about Sasha?"

The moment she mentioned his wife's name, he went rigid. He swallowed faintly, eyes darting to Forester, then back again. "I... I told you what happened," he said in a small whisper.

"I read the report, but I want to hear it from you."

He shrugged once. "I killed her." His voice trembled now. Grief flooded his tone as he repeated, in an even smaller voice, "I killed her."

He wasn't a good actor. His sleeping trick had proven that. So why did she believe the grief? The sadness. The absolute sound of regret in his voice.

"I checked your blood," she said quietly. She held up her phone, flashing the screenshot of a report. "It arrived a few minutes ago. You weren't drugged. Neither was Clarkson."

"Who is this Clarkson guy you keep mentioning?"

Artemis watched him closely. Still no sign of deception. What was she missing?

She said, "Why don't you tell me about the night your wife died?"

He dropped his head into his hands, his dark hair poking between his fingers. "Do I have to?" he murmured.

"Yes, please."

He shook his head. "What's the point? I already admitted it. I told you what I did."

"I'd like to hear it again. Were you two fighting?"

"No," he said.

"Was there a problem in your marriage?"

"No... We'd only been married a couple weeks."

Artemis leaned back now, crossing her arms, her fingers tingled from where they'd been touching the cold metal.

"So what happened that night?"

"We had dinner... We kissed. We were going to..." He glanced off to the side and shrugged. "Have some fun. Then someone knocked on the door."

"And then what?" Artemis asked. "Who was it?"

He paused now, his expression blank. "I... What?"

"Who knocked on the door?"

But again, it was as if he couldn't even compute the question. "Sorry, who are you?"

She stared at him, her skin prickling now. A slow, dawning realization came over her. She recognized, now, all of a sudden, the blank stare. The confusion. The nervous swallowing followed by a passage of time without any reaction at all.

But she needed to be sure. So she leaned in now, staring at him closely in the eye. Dilated. Calm pulse. Grief in his eyes, though. A tormenting mixture of placid and agitated.

This man was under hypnosis.

She should know—her father had been an expert hypnotist for years, as part of his mentalism act. Some people didn't believe hypnosis worked, and she would agree... to a point.

Hypnosis required trust and a willing mind. It required time.

To snap him out of it, though, she would need to know the anchoring phrase. Or the anchoring thought.

Hypnosis wasn't magic, but rather a psychological conditioning. The same way that if someone clicked their fingers in front of one's eyes, the other person would likely blink. There was no real threat to the eyes, but the instinctual reaction would cause the eyelids to shutter.

It was also like when someone looked *up* at the sky. They inadvertently would almost always keep their mouth suddenly wide open. It wasn't on purpose, but rather a deep-rooted instinct. One had to intentionally make an effort to keep their mouth closed while looking up at the sky or a tree.

But she didn't know the anchoring phrase. Didn't know the trigger.

But she knew a man under suggestion when she saw one. She leaned in so close now, that Forester cleared his throat. But she needed to unnerve him, to break a pattern he was expecting.

Ramirez frowned, leaning away from her, giving her a strange look.

"Can you hear me?" she said, staring at him, unblinking. "As in *really* hear me?"

He just stared back at her, a blank expression on his face. Artemis knew she had to try something else. She took a deep breath and decided to take a risk.

"Leo, listen to my voice. You're safe. You're not under hypnosis anymore. You can trust me."

She watched his expression closely, searching for any sign of recognition. But his face remained blank, and she began to worry that she might have made things worse.

She tapped him on the shoulder twice. Nothing happened. She leaned in, matching his breathing pattern, mirroring even the slightest of his movements.

"What happened to Sasha?" she said.

Suddenly, Ramirez's eyes widened, and he gasped. Artemis instinctively leaned forward, ready to catch him if he fell, but he simply grabbed her arm tightly.

"I killed her," he whispered. "I didn't mean to! I thought I was dreaming! I thought she was a wolf!"

Artemis bit her lip, trying to contain her excitement and horror. "What happened that night, Leo?"

He closed his eyes, shaking his head. "I don't want to remember. It was too painful."

"Please," she urged him. "You need to tell me. It's important."

Leo took a deep breath, hyperventilating now. He loosed a faint moan as his head wagged side to side. For a moment, he looked coherent, wide-eyed, but then, just as quickly as his eyes had cleared, a dark cloud seemed to descend over him.

He paused, only briefly, swallowed once, and whispered, "Oh... Okay then..."

Then suddenly he slammed his head against the table with a calamitous *thud!*

She yelled, reeling back at the sudden movement. He slammed his head against the table a second time, snarling as he did.

There was a clatter as Forester knocked over his chair, leaping across the table and extending a hand to catch the man's already bleeding forehead before it struck the metal again.

It all happened so quickly that Artemis didn't even have time to blink.

Forester's instincts, though, had taken over, and now he was holding Leo's head back, preventing it from slamming into the table once more.

Leo was sobbing, trembling terribly and trying to get away from Cameron.

"Calm down!" Forester was saying, gripping the back of the metal chair so Leo couldn't topple it. "What the hell just happened, Checkers? What'd you do?"

Leo's head was bleeding. Rivulets of red streamed down his brow, dripping past his eyes.

He was sobbing, and for a moment, it almost looked as if his tears were made of blood.

As Forester restrained the man, Artemis quickly darted into the hall, snatched the first-aid kit off the metal rack on the wall, and hastened back into the room, her skin buzzing. She approached the men where Leo looked to be slumped now in Forester's grasp.

With trembling fingers, cursing under her breath, Artemis took out some gauze and a disinfectant spray. She put on some gloves and gently sprayed the disinfectant on a piece of gauze, then carefully dabbed it on the wound.

"Leo, can you hear me?" she said, her voice calm and soothing. "You're safe. No one is going to hurt you."

Leo's sobs began to quiet down as he looked up at her with wide, frightened eyes. The blood was cleared but had left a rusty stain along his skin.

"What... what happened?" he asked, his voice shaking.

"You were under hypnosis," Artemis explained. "Someone has been manipulating your memories."

Leo's eyes widened in horror. But just as quickly, his eyes went distant again. "What did you say?" he asked.

Forester growled, "What's going on, Artemis?"

"He's in too deep," she said. "Any mention of hypnosis just makes him get violent or makes him forget. But someone else was there that night, Cameron. Someone knocked on the door." She was speaking quickly now, lowering the first aid kit and stepping back. Her skin prickled.

"Benjamin Clarkson was struck on the head by the door."

"What?"

"The front door. I think someone came to the door and triggered Benjamin."

"I... what? Like hypnotized him?"

"No. That would've happened a while ago. For something this deep? To kill someone they love?" Artemis was rattling it off now, watching the confused, blank expression on Leo's features. He was slumped again and pretending to sleep. She said, "Someone who knew him did this."

"Why? Who?"

"I don't know. But Leo does."

"Can you get him to... remember?"

She shook her head, hissing in frustration. "Not without the trigger phrase. The anchor, they call it. No. No, I can't."

"Shit, Artemis. So what now?"

Suddenly, Leo gasped again. He'd closed his eyes, his face contorting in pain. It looked to be taking him a great deal of effort to maintain his coherence. But he was now stammering as if answering a question from much earlier that had lagged before reaching him. "I... I don't know. It's all so confused. I remember... I remember feeling like I was dreaming. And then... and then I saw Sasha. And she was... she was a wolf."

Artemis stared at him. But he closed his eyes again and went silent.

The room suddenly went quiet. All Artemis could hear was the heavy breathing filling the space.

She stared at Forester and he stared back.

Benjamin Clarkson had also seemed odd. Also been blank-eyed and acted strangely.

The men had been hypnotized. Had been triggered into killing their own wives.

Someone with access to both men had set it up. Someone who'd knocked on the front doors to release the trigger, to cause the violence.

The only question was *who*?

Suddenly, there was a knocking sound on the door. A loud retort of knuckles on metal.

Then a voice barked into the interrogation room. "Agent Forester!"

"Busy!" Cameron called back.

The voice said, insistent, "There's another murder, sir. They found another body."

CHAPTER 9

Police cars were buzzing around at the bottom of the ravine, clogging up the single-lane road that cut through the mountain pass under the plateau upon which the vineyard sat.

Artemis stared down from her perch on the side of the road, one hand leaning against a gray railing, her eyes trailing along the valley floor.

"Can we get any closer by car?" she murmured, glancing towards where Forester was in a fierce conversation with one of the police blocking the road.

Forester just shook his head in frustration and continued speaking to the cop. "We need to get down there. *Now*! Move your asses out of the way."

The cop replied, and Artemis could tell tempers were rising, but she returned her attention to the valley floor.

Again, the body had plummeted off the cliff, striking stony teeth far below. A white tarp covered the body nearly a hundred feet below, creating a lump under the pale canvas.

Finally, Artemis began to walk, striding past the vehicles, moving quickly.

She didn't wait for Forester.

Dr. Bryant was back at the precinct, going over the physical evidence once again.

Artemis fingered the wedding ring in her pocket, feeling the nub of diamond against her palm.

She glanced up at the villa far above. Another murder.

But this time a man.

Noah Fieldgreen. And his wife Cynthia was still being interviewed. No confession yet.

Too much chaos.

Hypnosis was involved. Someone was enticing newlyweds to kill their loved ones. Something about the emotional resonance of a honeymoon—the new place, the new person... It lowered a malleable mind's guard.

Artemis shook her head, avoiding the front bumper of a silver SUV, sidestepping a couple of police officers standing by a sawhorse, then arriving at the side of the body under the tarp.

All around, forensic units were combing the terrain, searching for physical evidence.

And again, even through the thin tarp, Artemis noticed the way the body was posed.

Arms and legs were not splayed out but, rather, the hands were tucked under the head.

Posed as if sleeping.

She shivered, approaching the body, inhaling the scent of copper on the air, small rocks crunching underfoot.

As she crouched down next to the tarp, Artemis noticed something odd about the victim's hands. His fingers were twisted and curled unnaturally, visible just past the hem of the tarp, as if he had been clutching onto something tightly before he fell. She pulled back the covering slightly to get a better look and saw that the man's fingernails were broken and bloodied.

Artemis felt a knot form in her stomach. These weren't defensive wounds, as the cuts were along the back of the fingers. No... rather, it looked as if someone had dragged something metal across the hands... Pliers?

The ring was missing.

She could see the tan mark.

Another missing wedding ring. That made three.

She stood up quickly and turned to a nearby forensic technician. Part of her training for the field test had included a communications class. Normally, Artemis would request things politely, but it often backfired when people assumed she didn't know what she wanted, or what she was talking about.

So now, addressing the technician, she said, in a firm, clear voice, "Please get me a list of everyone who was at the vineyard today. We need to start interviewing witnesses."

The technician hesitated, glanced at her but then nodded and walked away quickly, leaving Artemis alone with the body. She took a deep breath and tried to ignore the sickening smell of blood and decay.

Something caught her eye and she leaned in closer. A small piece of paper was sticking out from under the victim's collar. She carefully removed it, trying not to disturb the body any further.

It was a note. Written in a shaky, panicked handwriting, it read.

I'm so sorry. I loved you.

Artemis felt a chill run down her spine.

Artemis folded the note carefully and put it in an evidence bag.

As she walked back up the ravine, she saw Forester waiting for her by the police cars. He looked agitated, and his jaw was clenched tightly.

"We need to get up to the villa. Cynthia Fieldgreen has something to tell us," he said, his voice low and urgent.

Artemis nodded and followed him to his car. They drove up the winding road to the villa, and Artemis felt a sense of unease settle over her. The sun was setting, casting eerie shadows over the sprawling structure. She knew that they were running out of time.

When they arrived at the villa, Cynthia Fieldgreen was waiting for them in the living room. She looked distraught, her eyes red-rimmed from crying.

"I didn't do it," she blurted out as soon as they entered the room. "Noah and I were happy. We were in love. Someone is trying to frame me."

Artemis studied Cynthia carefully. She seemed genuine, but she knew better than to trust appearances. She took a seat in a leather chair by a fireplace across from Cynthia and leaned in.

"I'm going to be honest with you," Artemis said quietly, "And I hope you'll repay the favor. We've had three murders like this in the last few weeks. Both other times, the spouse confessed to the murder."

She allowed the words to linger.

Cynthia looked panicked, swallowing slowly. She shook her head side to side. "I didn't do it! I didn't!"

She looked to be in shock, her eyes widening in horror.

Artemis glanced at the police officer standing sentry behind the spouse. The man shifted uncomfortably from one foot to the other.

Forester stood in the doorway, outlined by the sun.

Artemis returned her attention to the grieving widow.

"Cynthia, we need you to tell us everything you know. What happened this evening?"

"We were on a walk, coming home. That's all!"

"You don't seem too upset."

Cynthia gaped. "I'm horrified. In shock!"

Artemis hesitated briefly. The woman didn't look sad, but rather frightened. It was the look of someone intent on saving their own skin.

So Artemis said, "So if you were together, you saw him die?"

"No!" she replied adamantly.

"But you just said you two were walking home."

"I didn't see it happen."

"Alright... Let's try something else." Artemis leaned back in the chair. "Did your husband have any enemies?"

Cynthia shook her head. "No, nothing like that. Noah was a kind man." She wrinkled her nose. "A bit boring, I mean. But kind. We'd known each other since high school. He always had a crush on me, but... you know..." She snickered.

The sound didn't suit the situation. "He what?"

She tossed her hair with a flick of the wrist. "He was a pimply nerd. He wanted me—I knew that. But I didn't really care for him." She shrugged. Then, realizing how callous she must've sounded, she quickly tried to give a little gasp as if she'd been holding back a sob, but Artemis saw through the charade.

Forester was now watching the woman while wearing a strange expression. He picked up a small picture that had been resting on a stand by a red chair and held it up.

In the photo, it showed the recent victim and Cynthia kissing. They both looked content, happy, wrapped in each other's arms.

"You sure seem to like the guy here."

Cynthia snorted, waving a hand. "I mean..." she paused, then coughed and said, "Things change."

"What sort of things?" Artemis asked.

"Career, maybe?" Cameron said.

Artemis frowned at him.

But the tall man had paused by a dish near the window and fished out a set of keys. "New BMW," he said, emitting a low whistle. "And a place like this..." He spread his arms, indicating the room. "Doesn't come cheap, does it? Any chance the high school nerd came into some money, huh? Got a bit more attractive then, didn't he?"

Cynthia had gone quiet but was glaring at Forester. She shook her head. "I didn't hurt him! Why would I? Things were going great!

Besides, you just said, there were other murders here. It's someone else. You should be protecting *me*!" she said.

All the while, Artemis had been watching the woman closely. No sign of hypnosis. No sign of a foggy mind. She seemed lucid, and very angry.

Artemis frowned at this strange new development. The two others, both men, had shown signs of an external psychological influence.

But this woman just seemed angry.

Was she behind this all, somehow?

Artemis said, "Where were you last night?"

"W-what?"

"Last night—where?"

"Here, with my husband," she snapped back, clearly irritated now. "Why?"

Artemis shook her head. "Do you have proof of that?"

"Sure. A video of us together. You sure you want to see it?" Cynthia said, raising her eyebrows.

"Do you often take videos of yourself?" Forester asked. "Or just when you need an alibi?"

She looked at him and sneered, crossing her arms primly. "It's a career play, big guy." She studied him for a moment but then wiggled her eyebrows. "Does that attitude come with a bod?"

He blinked at her, surprised.

Then she just shook her head, saying, "We upload our videos online. We have a following. That's how the Kardashians made it, you know."

"I see," Artemis said. "We need to see the timestamps of those videos. Or we can request a warrant and do it officially back at a police station."

The woman looked hesitant but then shrugged. "Last night? Fine. Here."

She pulled out her phone, handing it towards Cameron. As he accepted it, she allowed her fingers to trail against his knuckles a bit too long.

He withdrew his hand quickly, cycling through the phone to check the videos. Artemis watched as he did, frowning at the woman.

She was being openly brazen, obnoxious, didn't seem to care her husband had died, and was showing no sign of foggy thinking or hypnosis.

This one didn't fit the pattern.

The murder victim was male as well...

So what was different? What had changed?

Briefly, she heard the sounds of moaning coming from the phone, and Cynthia tilted her head, not an ounce of embarrassment as Forester scrolled through the video.

He quirked an eyebrow as if amused at something but then shrugged, lowering the phone.

"Checks out," he said to Artemis. "She couldn't have been near the Clarkson villa. She was here. For a good few hours, too." He slipped the phone back onto the table next to the BMW keys.

Artemis was frowning now, ignoring Cynthia as she commented on Forester's muscled arms now. She was trying to bat her eyelashes at the man investigating her husband's murder.

Artemis looked away, glancing around the room.

Someone else had shown up at the Clarkson's villa, at the front door.

But if this woman had an alibi, why didn't she also show signs of hypnosis.

Artemis stood there for a moment, bit her lip, then said, "You're trying to blend in. Aren't you? This was a money play."

The woman blinked, staring at Artemis.

Forester also glanced over, looking curious.

"What are you talking about?" she demanded.

But Artemis was nodding now. She could see cracks in the facade. "You didn't have anything to do with Sasha and Gina's murders."

The woman nodded, smirking and settling back. "Of course not."

Artemis watched the woman's posture. Tightly gripped hands against her arms. Leaning back. Defensive postures. But a smug expression, a callous attitude. Clearly, the woman thought she was far too clever.

But clever doing what?

Artemis pictured past chess matches she'd had, sitting across from over-confident opponents. They thought they'd prepared their openings so perfectly, they didn't have a care in the world.

But Artemis was nodding now. She then turned to Forester. She didn't look at Cynthia any further. "She killed him."

"How's that?"

"She did it," Artemis said. "Not under compulsion, but to blend in."

Forester paused, raising an eyebrow. Out of the corner of her eye, Artemis spotted where Cynthia had gone still all of a sudden, sitting rigid in the seat.

But Artemis didn't look at her. Couldn't manage to bring herself to. Instead, she said, "Check the phone for this evening. Later. You won't find anything."

Forester reached for the phone slowly, but as he did, Cynthia's hand shot out, covering the phone.

She frowned at Forester then at Artemis.

But Artemis continued to ignore her. "She'll have videos and images throughout the day. Except from a couple of hours ago. She wouldn't have recorded it."

Forester pulled at the phone, but Cynthia didn't budge.

He pried her fingers off the device, tugged it towards himself, and began thumbing through.

The cop playing babysitter, behind the chair, looked uncomfortable at the way Forester was handling the device.

But Cameron had often played fast and loose with personal property laws.

Artemis was nodding to herself, her certainty growing.

Forester gave a low whistle, the screen illuminating his face as he stared down at the phone. "You're right. Nothing," he said. "No videos. No pictures. Nothing for the last two hours. An hour before your husband died," he said, turning to look back at Cynthia.

She'd changed now. All of a sudden, the look of confidence, of smugness had faded.

Instead, she now looked surprised, and even opened her mouth in something of a shocked expression. She held up her hand to her lips and began to tremble. Her pretty features bunched up into a crying face, and tears began leaking from her eyes.

"Ohmygosh," she whispered. "I... I'm in shock. I don't know... what's happening?"

Artemis nodded, impressed. "You really know how to turn it on, don't you? Is that how you suckered him into marrying you? A pouting lip and a pretty face go a long way, don't they?"

The woman's eyes flashed with rage.

But Artemis snorted in disgust. "She's a distraction," Artemis said, turning on her heel and moving towards the door.

The woman sitting there glared after her. Forester cleared his throat but didn't speak, clearly still hoping she'd fill in the blanks.

Artemis sighed, paused in the doorway, and looked back. She said, "She clearly heard about the other murders and wanted to use them as an excuse to kill her husband. She wants the money. It's as simple as that. I would explain how I know she's after the money, but I think we can all just *see* it, can't we? She also took his wedding ring off his hand. After she pushed him. Couldn't even give up the gold, could you? Did you hear in the news about the missing rings? Do you know someone on the police force?"

Each of Artemis' words seemed like a lash across the woman's face. She was staring, wide-eyed, expression gaunt.

The tears had vanished as well. Each time she communicated an expression, it was as if she were donning some new mask.

A sociopath, perhaps. Someone who'd used the tragedies in the mountains as an opportunity to get rid of her own husband. She'd married him for his money, and clearly saw no use in keeping him.

"He didn't sign a pre-nuptial, did he?" Artemis said quietly. "Hmm?"

The woman was sitting straight-backed, her teeth set, and Artemis could practically hear the gritting sound of teeth rubbing raw against each other.

She sighed, shaking her head and rubbing the bridge of her nose. "She has nothing to do with the other murders," Artemis said at last. "She's just a distraction."

"Hey!" the woman said sharply. "Hey—watch who you talk to like that! Do you know who I am?"

Artemis finally looked the woman directly in the eye. She held her gaze for a moment, then shook her head a single time. "No. No, I don't."

And then she turned to leave.

But just then, she heard a shout.

She whirled around, eyes wide. Cynthia's hands, which had been rigid at her sides, had fished something out of the slot in the cushion of the chair.

A gun.

A flash of silver as she raised it, screaming. She pointed it at Artemis and squeezed the trigger.

CHAPTER 10

Artemis only had time to register the shock as the gun fired. Cynthia's face had twisted into a mask of rage.

But Forester moved just as quickly.

The large man was a step too far to reach her or to grab the gun. So instead, as she pulled the trigger, Artemis watched, as if in slow motion, as the ex-fighter planted a foot and spun on his back heel.

He kicked out with his other foot, catching the gun just as it fired.

The spinning back kick knocked the gun off target. It fired, the bullet striking the chandelier over the stairwell, smashing glass baubles and sending them scattering to the ground in a shower of glass-like hailstones.

Cynthia screeched, trying to aim again, but this time, Forester had closed the distance.

In a move too fast for Artemis to track, the lanky agent swept in, disarmed the woman, and knocked her back onto the couch.

Then his cuffs appeared in one hand, and with a snarl, he snatched her wrist, cuffing her faster than she could react.

"You stupid bitch!" Cynthia was screaming now. "You don't know anything! I didn't do it! I didn't! You moron!"

Artemis was breathing rapidly, rooted to the spot, her skin prickling as fear coursed through her body. Her hands trembled and she tucked them into her pockets to hide the shaking.

She was very pale as it was, but she imagined her pallor had only grown more ghostly. Sweat prickled along the insides of her hands as she stood rooted to the spot.

It had all been a distraction. A crime of opportunity. Cynthia had wanted to blend in with the other murders. But for money. Simple as that.

Now, cuffed, she was spitting and trying to kick at Forester's shins. The agent shoved the handcuffed woman to the cop behind the couch, who'd reacted slower. The man had cuffs out as well but was red-faced as if embarrassed.

Forester pointed a thick finger at the man and snarled, "Check for guns next time, asshole. She's your problem."

Then, Cameron spun on his heel, moving away, approaching Artemis, and looking her up and down, wearing an expression of concern.

"I'm fine," she said quickly, her breath labored. "Really. I'm fine."

She turned, still hiding her shaking hands as she moved towards the door.

"That was close," Forester muttered, walking behind her. "Too damn close. Sorry. I... I wasn't paying attention. Dammit." He snarled under his breath, and she spotted him striking his own leg with a closed fist.

They stepped outside the villa, and she reached out, touching his arm where he kept his fist bunched. "It's not your fault," she whispered. "I agitated her. I should've been more careful."

But Forester wasn't listening. His eyes were dark, cloudy, as if a storm was brewing.

He couldn't seem to even notice the scenic views beyond the villa. Didn't look at the trees or the valleys or the slopes.

Instead, he stood like a shadow, his motions and movements tied up in those of another.

He kept shaking his head, his shoulders tense.

"I nearly lost you again," he muttered.

Again.

She realized now, as he had in the past, Forester wasn't looking at her. He saw someone else. He was talking to someone from his past.

This time, though, strangely, she found it didn't bother her as much.

Perhaps it was because she'd grown used to it.

Or maybe it was because...

Her eyes widened. "Memory recollection."

"What?"

"I... If the two men were hypnotized, that means the memories could be retrieved even without breaking the hypnosis. It would just require substitute anchors."

"What do you mean?"

But Artemis was biting her lip, wringing her hands. "I... I don't know how to do it."

"You don't?"

"No. But..." She froze in place, stunned that she was about to say what she had in mind. "But I know someone who can. Someone who's an excellent mentalist."

"Who?"

"Just..." She swallowed. "A friend."

Her mind was spinning now. Her father was meant to lay low, to hide. But he was with her brother in Seattle, only a couple hour's drive away.

He had been growing antsy, stir-crazy sitting around all day. Eventually, she suspected, he'd try to sneak away.

Her father was still wanted for murder.

He had escaped prison thanks to her, but now... now he was growing restless.

Besides, if anyone could pass themselves as something else, it was a practiced liar like her old man. The idea of asking him for anything, not long ago, would've made her skin crawl.

But the guilt still weighed heavy on her. She could feel it like stones in her intestines, weighing her down.

She'd doubted her father's innocence.

But in the end, it had turned out that he'd taken the conviction out of love for Helen.

Her father had been willing to go to prison to protect his oldest daughter.

But he'd always maintained his innocence, and Artemis had never believed him... to her shame.

She bit her lip now, causing a flash of pain.

Perhaps it was the effect of nearly being shot, or maybe it was the sense of duty and responsibility she felt towards Dr. Bryant after everything the coroner had done for Artemis.

But she nodded to herself, pulled her phone from her pocket, and began moving away.

"Where are you going?"

"Nowhere. Just... give me a second. I have to make a call."

CHAPTER 11

Artemis sat alone on the bluff, at the top of a winding trail, waiting nervously in the front of the car.

Technically, she'd snuck the keys from Forester's jacket pocket back at the villa without telling him where she was going.

But she'd guessed that for *this,* she couldn't allow witnesses.

The mountain slopes, the darkening night, and the glower of the moon all filled her with a strange sense of unease, though. She could feel her stomach doing flips. Could feel her skin prickling as she felt exposed.

A dream about a wolf...

And then he'd killed his wife.

A wolf?

She thought, in the distance, earlier, she'd even heard the howl of one such creature.

She shivered as she considered it, turning to stare through the windshield once more, down the trail.

She glanced at the red digits of the clock on the dashboard, drumming her fingers on the steering wheel.

Her father was late.

Raindrops had started now. The evening sky had become corpulent and now the thick, gray clouds shed their burden.

A steady tap-tap-tap echoed through the vehicle.

And then she spotted headlights. The crunching sound of asphalt being displaced by rubber wheels. A car was turning up the switchback further down the road.

She stared, her own headlights dim. Her hands clutched the steering wheel.

The last time she'd been alone at night with her father had been the night she'd helped him escape.

Now, she wondered if she'd made a mistake.

What if... what if it wasn't her father?

What if the FBI had intercepted the phone call?

Suddenly, she stared at the approaching vehicle with a rising sense of fear.

The SUV was sleek, new. Tinted windows. The sort of car the feds might drive.

Now, every instinct in her, every synapse firing told her to bolt. To flee.

A trap.

A trap she'd set for herself.

But she remained seated, refused to budge, summoning what inner resolve she had.

She stared as the car continued up towards her, trundling slowly along.

Her brother worked for the mob. He'd have access to vehicles like this too.

Then, the car came to a stop.

She stared.

Swallowed.

It faced her. The headlights facing hers, like some sort of buck, lowering its horns, threatening an intruder.

She still felt the desire to flee. But now, the SUV was blocking her egress.

Then, the front door opened.

It swung out in the rain, the glass slick with droplets slaloming down the tinted surface.

A figure stood there. A figure she didn't recognize. A chubby man with round cheeks and a hooked nose. He had disheveled hair, and dull, gray eyes.

He stared at her, blinking a few times and rubbing at the back of his pudgy fingers.

He took a tentative step forward then winced as if the rain was hurting him, paused, ducked back inside the vehicle, and emerged with a magazine, which he held up and over his head, blocking the raindrops.

Then the man moved towards her. He seemed to have a faint limp in his right leg, and his movements were slow, encumbered by his bulk.

Water droplets slicked his cheeks, his forehead, and he kept reaching up, brushing aside the rain with hairy knuckles.

Her heart was in her throat, but as the man drew closer, she rolled down her window.

"Nice disguise," she said, her voice still shaking but some of the fear depleting.

The strange man, who looked completely unfamiliar, blinked a couple of times. Then his face broke into a grin.

"How'd you know it was me?" He gave a little twirl, like a ballerina, suddenly moving far more animatedly than he had earlier.

She pointed. "The magazine. People don't read magazines anymore. Your prison years are showing."

Then, she bit her tongue, realizing how insensitive it had sounded. "Umm... sorry, I was just trying to make an observation."

He waved away her apology, though, and slipped into the front seat next to her.

The door shut, and it echoed through the car with a strange finality.

For a moment, the two of them sat in complete silence. She glanced over at her father once more. "Prosthetic cheeks?"

"Mhmm. Like 'em?"

"Can't say I do. But I shouldn't have been worried—you're right. No one's going to recognize you. Even the way you walk..."

"Yeah. I've had practice. Thanks for calling me up here, kiddo."

"Yeah."

Again, they drifted off into silence. Artemis could feel her stomach turning. It was uncomfortable for her, sitting here, not quite looking at her father who didn't look familiar at all.

Her father was normally a handsome man, with curling blonde hair and an overconfident posture.

Now, though, he looked like some dockyard construction worker or a deli owner.

He even smelled faintly of pastrami.

"So," he said, breaking the awkward silence at last, "What's this problem you have?"

She turned to him, nodding, grateful to be able to focus on work. It was just too weird to dwell on the situation itself.

She lowered her hands from the steering wheel, rubbing at her fingers as if to get the blood flowing.

As she did, she said, "Hypnosis subjects. Two of them. They both murdered their wives. They're in deep."

Her father blinked. "Newlyweds?"

"Yeah."

"Makes sense. More susceptible to manipulation when in heightened states."

"Yeah."

He shook his head. "Still... To kill their own wives?"

"Yes. I know. A big ask."

"Impossible, really." Her father was shaking his head. "It's not really possible to push someone to do something they wouldn't normally do. Hypnosis is an inhibition remover more than anything. Only the

116

most pliable minds would be willing to go under for something like that..."

She frowned. "So you're saying it's not hypnosis?"

"I'm not saying that. I'm just saying that it's a strange case. I'd have to speak with the subjects."

"Not possible. They're in a jail cell."

"I don't think I can be much help then."

Abruptly, and without warning, her father began to push open the door and to walk back to the SUV.

Artemis huffed in frustration. He often pulled shit like this, but she kept her temper in check and said, "Hang on. Hang on... Maybe we can do something. But I don't know how to get you in."

He turned back to her, shutting the door again, and sending the fragrance of rainwater sweeping through the car.

He pulled a badge from his pocket, flashing it towards her. "Special Agent Jeremy Greeves," he said simply. He grinned, revealing two golden teeth replacements.

She shook her head, staring. "You... want to impersonate a federal officer?"

He grinned at her. "I'm already serving six life sentences, Artemis. Do you want my help or not?"

She shivered, sitting alone on the bluff in the car with her father.

A man she'd trained herself to despise. Nearly two decades of assuming his guilt, of contemplating the murders he'd committed, but in the end, it had turned out to be her sister's doing.

Artemis swallowed, her voice hoarse as she said, "How's Helen?"

"Doing well. She misses you."

A pang jolted through Artemis' chest. She lowered her eyes, staring at the dark opening under the steering wheel. She let out a faint sigh and looked up again. "Is she... who's..."

"In control?"

Artemis bit her lip and nodded. Her sister Helen suffered from a split personality disorder. The Ghost Killer and Helen both shared the same body. They'd been at war with each other for years.

"Helen left to protect you," her father said simply. "She didn't want to put you in harm's way, so she left."

"It was a mistake," Artemis cut in quickly. "She should've stayed."

"Yeah. Probably. That's the hope isn't it?" Her father leaned back, rubbing at his soft chin prosthetic. "Isolating herself was the mistake. With us... she can live a normal life."

"Yeah. That's the hope. She will," Artemis added quickly. "She has to."

A bleak mood had come over the car, and again they drifted into silence. Helen had been at war with this other part of herself for decades. Artemis hadn't known. Her father had kept it a secret from the other siblings.

She couldn't blame him...

But Artemis' memories of Helen were fond. Helen had been on medication while under their roof, and it had helped her survive.

But then she'd left... And she'd stopped taking them.

Now, she was back on the medication. Back with her family.

Safe.

For now.

But Artemis wasn't sure how safe the rest of them were. Still... she refused to give up on her sister.

She wouldn't make the same mistake she had with her father.

Family was all she had left in a way.

Jamie was gone.

A flare of grief.

She shook her head, feeling her skin tingling along her back. She said, slowly, "Alright... If you have to speak with them in person, I can get you a meeting with one of them. A guy named Benjamin Clarkson.

He pushed his wife off a bluff and then posed her body at the base of the canyon."

"Okay." Her father frowned. "Alright. I'll see what I can find. But Artemis?"

"Yeah."

"No promises. I don't know what we're dealing with here. Hypnosis is a tricky thing."

"Yeah, well... Impersonating a federal officer is also tricky," she muttered. She shook her head side to side, wondering how on earth things had grown so strange in her life.

Her father let out a low chuckle all of a sudden. Memories came back of that same, self-confident, humorous sound. "We'll make it work. We always do."

Artemis gave a small smile, feeling the tension in the car dissipate slightly. She didn't quite trust her father. Despite everything. But she knew he had her back.

They drove back down the bluff in silence, the sound of rain pounding against the roof of the car. Artemis couldn't help but feel a sense of unease settling in her stomach.

The case with the hypnotized murderers was a strange one, and she couldn't shake the feeling that there was more to it than met the eye. In the distance... was that another wolf's howl? Or was she just being paranoid?

As they pulled up to the nearly abandoned precinct parking lot, Artemis' nerves began to fire. She stared towards the illuminated, sliding glass doors, expecting a host of cops to come charging out and arrest them both at any moment. Her father, on the other hand, seemed calm and cool and collected. He turned to her. "You need to be in the room too."

"Okay... Why?" Artemis unbuckled her seatbelt, reaching for the door handle.

"Because... tampering with a hypnotist's work, especially with violence involved, could yield... *unpredictable* results. Like I said, I don't know what we're dealing with here."

She turned back to him, meeting his gaze. "What sort of unpredictable results?" Her skin tingled. "Could he get violent?"

Her father nodded once. "A distinct possibility. His dull, gray eyes—created by contact lenses—stared out from his foam and make-up-altered features.

He stared at her briefly, swallowed, then reached out. Artemis had been pushing open her door, forcing herself not to succumb to fear, but his hand grazed her arm, and she turned back looking at him.

For the faintest moment, she almost thought she spotted tears in his eyes.

She went still. Startled.

Her father said, quietly, "Thanks for asking me here. It means a lot."

She shifted uncomfortably. It wasn't like this was some sort of father-daughter outing, but he was treating it like one.

Still... she supposed after fifteen years in prison, her father had a right to make meaning from even the small things in life.

"I'm sorry for everything," her father said suddenly, speaking the words quickly, as if ripping off a band-aid.

Artemis felt her heart clench at the apology. It was a rare moment of vulnerability from her father, and she knew it wasn't easy for him to say.

"I know," she said softly. "I forgive you." She thought of the lies. The pretense. The concealing.

But then she said, "I'm sorry. Really sorry."

He nodded once and gave her a small smile, and then he turned, pushing open the door and stepping out into the rain. This time, he left the magazine behind.

Her father was always excellent at perfecting his little performances.

The king of deception, some called him.

But this time, he was on her side.

And if anyone could figure out what had happened to Benjamin Clarkson, to Leo Ramirez, it was her father.

She watched as he seamlessly slipped back into the jolting limp. His shoulders hunched just a bit. His head dipped and thrust forward.

He looked world-weary, exhausted all of a sudden. but also confident, authoritative.

For a brief moment, she just watched, impressed.

Her father was the best there was.

No one could lie with their body language nearly as well as he could.

But then, as she slipped out of the car, the unease returned.

What did her father mean about needing her in the room?

What was he expecting Benjamin to do?

She shivered, frowning at where her father took the steps to the police precinct.

Small, cold droplets of water struck her cheeks, and she hastened forward, after him.

Would the cops stop them?

Would they recognize her father?

So many questions. So many worries. What was Benjamin going to do if her father pushed him too far?

Hell, what was going on here? Who was killing these women, using the men like puppets?

And would they kill again?

It was this last thought that gave her the final jolt of courage to push forward, following her father up the steps and into the mountainside precinct.

CHAPTER 12

He stroked the beast's fur in slow, intentional motions, feeling the coarse prickle along his extended fingers.

He had soft fingers. These were not the hands of a laborer.

Nor the scent.

He could detect the fragrance of his own cologne. He sat in the comfortable armchair, facing his client.

He continued to stroke the wolf's fur as he did.

The man sitting across from him looked half asleep, his eyes hooded, his arms limp at his sides.

"Is it over?" whispered the client, his voice shaking briefly.

But the psychologist just smiled, shaking his head side to side. He continued to stroke the animal's fur.

Of course, he didn't tell his clients it was a wolf.

They all thought it was a therapy dog—some sort of husky.

But that's because people never looked close enough.

The psychologist enjoyed this part of the sessions most of all.

He was in full control.

His client had come in, nervous and excited. His guard down. Spilling all of his secrets.

It was amazing what a degree on a wall could entice someone to entrust with you.

Now, the client's head was dipping lower, his eyes still closed.

The psychologist continued to pet the wolf. The creature sat still by the side of the reclining chair, motionless, like a sentry. The psychologist had trained the animal himself.

He could train all sorts of animals.

The man glanced around the room and noted the small details—the old-fashioned velvet curtains that hung from the windows, the worn and threadbare furniture, the paintings that depicted a variety of gothic scenes. He adjusted the back of his chair and leaned in towards his client, a man in his mid-thirties who had a look of apprehension and fear on his face.

The psychologist smiled and said, "Well then, shall we finish?"

The client nodded but didn't speak. His eyes suddenly widened briefly. A flare of emotion in his eyes. His gaze darted around the room as if searching for an escape. The psychologist could sense the man's tension, as if he were trying to resist the process.

"Relax," the psychologist said in a soothing tone. "Let your body sink into the chair and your mind drift away. Think of nothing but my voice."

The man closed his eyes and began to take slow, deep breaths. The psychologist continued to speak in a low, monotone voice, repeating the same words over and over. He spoke of a place of safety, of peace and relaxation. As the man grew more and more relaxed, the psychologist increased the intensity of his voice, adding words of suggestion.

"Remember," he was saying. "Remember the dreams. Can you remember the dreams? Remember the dreams."

The repeated cadence of the words, the slow monotone had a soothing effect.

The man was no longer glancing around.

Once more, he'd fallen back into a trance.

The client's breathing became slower and more shallow as he slowly succumbed to the process. The psychologist smiled in satisfaction as he watched his client slowly slip away into a trance-like state.

After what seemed like an eternity, the man's eyes opened and he was fully hypnotized. The psychologist knew that now it was time to give the client his command.

"You will obey my every command," he said firmly. "You will do whatever I ask of you, without hesitation or question. Do you understand?"

The man nodded, his face completely void of emotion.

"Good," the psychologist said. "Now... you don't want her to get hurt, do you? That's why you came here. You want to be a good husband, don't you?"

"Mhmm..." A low mumble, a faint nod.

"Good... Good. You need to protect her, then. Protect her right now!"

The client looked frightened all of a sudden. "Protect her..." he repeated, his jaw slack.

The psychologist leaned back, smiling and nodding. He removed his hand from the wolf, no longer stroking the creature's fur.

The animal hesitated, then began to growl, irritated by the interruption in the grooming.

The growl turned to a rumble, filling the space. The faint aroma of incense wafted on the air. The psychologist's eyes never left his client.

The man just stared blankly at the psychologist, unsure of how to respond.

"Do you understand?" the psychologist repeated.

Finally, the man nodded. "Yes... yes, I have to protect her." He was sounding more frightened now.

The wolf's growl was resonating, rumbling through the room.

"Do you hear that? Do you hear the threat?"

The man nodded slowly. "I hear it."

"What is it?"

"Danger!"

"Yes... and what do we do with danger?"

"Stop it. Protect her."

"Yes, yes. Protect her!" The psychologist said, his voice rising in excitement. He stood from his chair all of a sudden, his shadow cast towards his client like the wings of a bat unfurling.

The man stared down at his subject, feeling a shiver of delight course through his frame.

"The wolf will come for her," said the psychologist. "And you must save her. Take the wolf, throw it off the cliff! Kill the wolf!"

"Kill the wolf," the man repeated in a low, dull voice.

The psychologist nodded firmly. The wolf continued to growl, and then keen softly. The growling turned to a faint but soft howl, more like a moan. Its deep-throated ululations filling the room.

"Protect her at all costs. No matter what. Throw the beast off the cliff. Then help the beast sleep. Just like we've been talking about. Does that make sense?"

The client was too sleepy, in too deep to respond. But he nodded, eyes still half-hooded, stuck in his trance.

They'd been meeting for weeks now.

Weeks of access.

Weeks of unfettered trust.

Now, the client was finally under his spell.

The psychologist smiled, satisfied with his work.

He had broken a man.

Shaped him, honed him into a tool.

The psychologist turned now, glancing at the portrait on his wall.

His eyes flashed.

A painting.

Of himself.

A child.

And a headless woman.

The head had been gouged out by a knife. Removed from the painting.

He glared at the item, turned back, and said, "Leave now. Go protect your wife."

The man pushed off the couch, nodding fiercely.

And as the wolf continued to growl behind him, he moved hastily towards the door, hands white-knuckled at his side, fear evident in his posture.

Chapter 13

Artemis' stomach was filled with butterflies as she pushed open the door to the interrogation room. The cop inside was busy locking the handcuffs through the metal ring on the table.

He glanced at Artemis and said, "Is that all, Agent Blythe?"

She flashed a quick smile, nodding. "Thanks."

Of course, she wasn't an agent, but she'd allowed the on-duty sergeant to assume so. He'd recognized her from when she'd first come with Forester.

It had been surprisingly easy to get access to the prisoner.

Now, the cop checked the handcuffs, rattling them, nodded, and moved away.

"I'll be at the desk if you two need anything."

She nodded then stepped aside as her father brushed past her, moving into the room.

Her father reached out, catching the arm of the cop as he was leaving.

Artemis' heart skipped a bit. She froze. She'd explicitly told her father not to bring any attention to himself.

But now, he was gripping the man's wrist and looking him in the eye.

Artemis' heart pounded wildly.

The cop turned back, frowning at the self-professed agent.

Her father's fake combover ruffled in the current of air from the vents above. He flashed a golden-toothed smile in his altered face and said, in a sibilant voice, "Some coffee would be nice. Black. No sugar."

The cop frowned, glancing at Artemis.

She winced apologetically. "It's fine. We don't need anything."

"I really must insist," her father cut in.

The desk sergeant sighed, shook his head, but then turned, muttering, "Give me a sec."

He then beat a hasty retreat, shutting the door behind him.

Artemis glared at the side of her father's face. "So much for not drawing attention to yourself," she whispered fiercely.

But her father replied also in a soft voice. "The best way to get people to stop scrutinizing you? Make them feel insecure. A man focused inwards misses the obvious outwards details."

Artemis blinked. Now that she thought about it, her father's choice made some small sense.

But then she frowned, watching as he limped across the room, approaching the table with his hunched form.

A part of her suspected her father had simply wanted coffee and was now bullshitting her.

Still... they were in the room.

And they were facing the hypnotized murderer.

Benjamin Clarkson sat in the metal chair, his hands cuffed, his hair disheveled.

He looked miserable.

Artemis approached as well. She stood at the table as her father took a seat. He made a big effort of dragging the metal chair back, to make room for his stomach padding.

He then rested his hands on the table, staring across it towards the suspect.

"Benjamin," her father said quietly.

The suspect looked over. Now that he did, Artemis could see the similarities in his features to his sister.

Dr. Bryant had the same caring eyes. Had the same gentle features. Kind features.

This was not the expression of a murderer. He looked as if he'd been through hell and back. His shoulders were slumped, his posture stooped, his expression haggard.

Artemis felt a jolt of sympathy. She checked her phone quickly where Dr. Bryant had been texting her.

The last text had simply read, *I don't know what to think...*

Artemis felt her heart pang. She returned her attention to the table.

If anyone could figure out what had happened, it was her father.

Now she watched as her old man settled, mirroring the suspect's slouched posture.

In a clear, crisp voice, her father said, "Why don't you tell me what matters most to you?"

It was an odd question.

But Artemis knew better than to doubt her father's methods.

Benjamin looked similarly confused. He swallowed, blinked a couple of times, then muttered, "S-sorry, what?"

"What matters most to you, Benjamin?" her father repeated. "Is it your family? Your friends? Your freedom?"

Benjamin's eyebrows furrowed as he thought about the question. "I... I don't know."

Artemis leaned forward slightly, intrigued. Her father had always been good at getting people to open up.

"What about Dr. Bryant?" her father asked, mentioning Benjamin's sister. "Does she matter to you?"

Benjamin's expression shifted, his eyes growing distant. "Yes. Yes, she does."

"Why is that?"

"She's... she's the only family I have left," Benjamin replied, his voice breaking slightly. "After our parents died, it was just the two of us. She's always been there for me."

Artemis felt a pang of sympathy for Benjamin. Losing one's parents was hard enough, but to be accused of murder on top of it...

Her father nodded, his expression thoughtful. "I see. And what about the night of the murder? Can you tell us what happened then?"

Benjamin's face fell, his eyes flickering with fear. "I... I don't remember. I was drunk. I blacked out."

Artemis watched as her father leaned forward, his voice firm, unyielding. He said, "You weren't drunk."

It wasn't a question.

"I wasn't."

"But you did black out."

A nod.

"And you dreamed."

Benjamin went still now, his expression going blank.

Her father looked suddenly excited, leaning in. He stared at the man, nodding fiercely. "That's it... right there. I see you," he whispered under his breath.

Benjamin didn't react. His eyes were hooded now.

Her father said, "Listen to my voice, Benjamin. Listen to nothing but my voice."

His eyes were shifting back and forth now, moving side to side. He didn't want to meet her father's gaze.

Artemis remembered her father's warning. She had to be in the room in case something happened.

But what?

What had he been frightened of?

"Who did this?" her father said. "No, don't look away. Look at me. Listen to my voice. Just my voice."

Artemis watched in awe as her father spoke in a low, soothing voice. His words seemed to penetrate Benjamin's defenses, and she could see his face relaxing, his eyes growing distant once again.

"Who did this?" her father repeated. "You know who did this. Tell me. Tell me everything."

Benjamin's mouth opened, but no sound came out. He shook his head as if trying to shake off the hypnotic trance her father had put him in. But her father wasn't letting go.

"Who did this?" he said again, his voice growing more insistent. "You saw their face. You know who did this. Tell me who it was."

And then, Benjamin's mouth started moving, his voice low and hesitant. "It was... it was a man. I didn't see his face. But he was tall... and muscular. He... he had a tattoo on his arm. A dragon."

Artemis felt her heart race as she listened to Benjamin's words. This was a breakthrough. They finally had a lead, a clue to follow.

"Good," her father said, his voice still low and insistent. Then, for a brief moment, he hesitated. He frowned, leaned forward, and clicked his fingers.

Benjamin didn't blink.

Her father leaned back, scowling now.

"What is it?" she whispered.

But he just shook his head. "Tell me again who did this?" her father said.

"It was a woman. She was angry at me. Bitter. She had red hair."

Her father crossed his arms now. He repeated the question. "Who did this?"

"It was a trucker. He stopped by the house and asked for help to jump his stalled vehicle. The guy had long hair. A pony-tail."

Each time Benjamin replied, it was with complete sincerity.

Her father looked at Artemis, giving a faint shake of his head. "He's locked in."

"What's that mean?"

"I can try to brute force it, but we'll have consequences if I'm wrong."

She shifted uncomfortably, glancing back towards the door. The sergeant hadn't returned with the coffee. She supposed it was good he hadn't come back.

Now, though, without waiting for her go-ahead, her father stood up, fast and quick. He started speaking, his voice louder.

"Listen to my voice. Don't listen to anyone else. Hey! Hey! Pay attention." Her father slapped a hand against the table, in a sort of rhythmic pattern.

Whenever she suffered panic attacks, a similar staccato sound helped her to focus, to give her mind something to concentrate on.

Now, her father continued to slap the table, standing tall, facing the man in the chair.

Benjamin began to shake, to tremble. He went still.

"Tell me who did this," her father said. "Remember your wife? Remember what happened?"

Suddenly, Benjamin's posture shifted.

One moment, he'd been leaning back as if trying to escape. He'd shrunk in on himself, trying to make himself small, unnoticeable.

But then, all of a sudden, his eyes flared. He went rigid.

The calm, gentle expression from those kind eyes shifted. There was a panic in his gaze.

"Don't hurt her!" Benjamin screamed suddenly. Spittle flew from his lips, scattering across the table. "No! NO! Don't hurt her! Get back! Get back you beast!"

Artemis's heart leapt into her throat as Benjamin's outburst filled the room. Her father had warned her that there could be consequences if he was wrong, but she hadn't expected this. She watched in horror as Benjamin's body convulsed, his eyes rolling back into his head.

"Benjamin, can you hear me?" her father said, his voice low and soothing once again. "Listen to my voice. Just my voice. You're safe. No one is going to hurt you."

But Benjamin didn't seem to hear him. He continued to thrash around in the chair, his body contorting in unnatural ways.

"Shouldn't we call a doctor or something?" Artemis said, her voice trembling.

"No," her father replied firmly. "This is beyond medical help. I have to break the trance."

"How?"

But before he could answer, Benjamin's body went still. His eyes flickered open, and he looked around the room as if seeing it for the first time.

"What... what happened?" he said, his voice hoarse.

Artemis let out a breath she didn't know she'd been holding. "You were hypnotized," she said, her voice gentle. "Do you remember anything?"

Benjamin shook his head. Then his eyes widened, staring in horror at her father.

"G-gina?" he whispered. "GINA! NO!"

And suddenly, Benjamin surged up and forward. His hands yanked at the cuffs, and something cracked.

He pulled his hand *through* the cuffs. A thumb broken.

But he managed to yank his arm free.

The cuffs dangled uselessly as they slid from the iron ring.

Benjamin snarled now then lunged across the table with a desperate shout.

His hands extended like claws, lurching towards her father, fury in his eyes, his screeching voice piercing the room like a knife.

CHAPTER 14

As Benjamin lunged at him, ignoring his broken finger and the dangling cuffs, her father tried to stumble back, but like Artemis, his skills were more of the mental variety.

He stumbled, and Benjamin landed on top of him.

Miracle's brother wasn't speaking but, rather, was spluttering, snarling, and making sounds like some animal. He was on top of Otto Blythe, choking the man's neck.

Artemis stumbled forward, trying to push him off.

But Benjamin was too strong, fueled by an unknown rage. He pushed her away with ease, his eyes locked onto her father's.

"Stop it, Benjamin!" Artemis shouted, her voice desperate. "Please, stop!"

Her hands pushed at his back, but he was like a solid brick wall. Some hidden strength summoned all of a sudden.

"Don't hurt her!" Benjamin was screaming. "Don't hurt her, please!"

Artemis tried to pry him off her father, but he threw out an arm, sending her stumbling back again.

Benjamin continued to choke her father, his hands tightening around the man's neck.

Artemis looked around frantically, searching for something to help her. And then she saw it.

The metal chair.

Without hesitation, Artemis grabbed the chair from the spot by the table and swung it with all her might. It connected with Benjamin from behind.

He yelped, lurching forward, off her father now.

Otto was gasping, his face red. He tried to struggle away, slipped once, but then, panting and hastily adjusting his prosthetic nose, which had come off in the fight, he regained his feet and darted around the table, putting it between himself and Benjamin Clarkson.

With him on the other side of the table, this left Artemis holding the metal chair, facing Benjamin on her own.

He was staring at her, blinking, eyes wide, nostrils flared. He breathed heavily, looking confused.

"Calm down!" Artemis was saying. "Please, calm down."

But he was shaking his head, spittle dripping down his lips now. He was in deep.

Artemis had a brief moment where her mind wandered—she'd never seen such strong hypnosis before. Whoever had done this to him, whoever had tampered with his mind had gone deep.

She tried to hold the chair between the two of them. He was staring at the jutting, metal legs as if they were a phalanx of spearmen. He moved to the right, but she blocked him. He moved to the left, and she followed, her feet shuffling along the ground, her breath coming in fierce gasps.

"Don't! Please don't!" she said.

But, though he stared at her, it was as if he couldn't hear her. He was still whispering, like some sort of mantra, "Don't hurt her. Please, don't hurt her!"

"Benjamin! You're dreaming! Snap out of it!"

But her words fell on deaf ears. Benjamin's eyes were locked onto her, his body tense and ready to pounce. The panic in his gaze had given way to a terrifying determination.

Artemis had to think fast. She couldn't let Benjamin hurt her or her father. She had to break the hypnosis, but how?

And then she remembered something her father had once told her about hypnosis. It wasn't the words themselves that put someone under, it was the rhythm and cadence of the voice.

With that in mind, Artemis began to hum a tune, a tune that her father used to sing to her when she was a child. It was a soothing melody, a lullaby.

As she did it, she instantly felt silly...

But she wasn't like Cameron. She couldn't beat up a room full of bad guys.

And so, her lips buzzing, feeling silly, she hummed.

At first, Benjamin didn't seem to notice, his eyes still locked onto her. But then, slowly, his body began to relax. His breathing slowed, and he blinked several times.

Artemis kept humming, her voice soft and gentle. She could feel the tension in the air easing.

At last, Benjamin's eyes drifted away from her, and he looked around the room as if seeing it for the first time.

"What..."

Artemis began to lower the chair. Her father whispered, "Are you okay, Art?"

The moment he spoke, though, Benjamin stiffened. His eyes landed on her once more.

He froze.

It was in that moment, Artemis realized just *how* deeply his mind was possessed by the thoughts of another.

He stood frozen to the ground, staring at her, slack-jawed.

And then the rage returned.

Something had triggered it. When she'd lowered the chair? The motion? The question from her father?

Too late to consider.

Benjamin charged at her, his hands extended like claws once again. Artemis lifted the chair to defend herself, but he was too quick. He knocked it out of her hands with a swipe and tackled her to the ground.

Artemis hit the hard floor with a thud, her head spinning. Her vision was blurry, but she could see Benjamin's crazed face looming over her.

"Please, Benjamin," she whispered, tears streaming down her face. "Please don't! It's just a dream!"

But he didn't seem to hear her. He had a look of pure insanity in his eyes.

Suddenly, there was a loud bang.

The door to the interrogation room swung open.

Everyone turned, even Benjamin. They all stared at the figure standing in the doorway like a pink-and-purple-haired avenging angel with paste-on eyelashes.

Her white coroner's jacket fluttered around her, carried by the air conditioning breeze in the hall.

Her eyes were fixated on her brother, and she stood stout and strong, her heavy bosom protruding out as she jutted her chest, her hands at her side in fists.

"Benjamin, don't!" Dr. Miracle Bryant called out.

Artemis' father was still cowering behind the table, even though his daughter was on the ground. Artemis scrambled to her feet now, gasping heavily, anxiety swirling in her stomach.

She beat a hasty retreat behind the table with her father.

Now, she wished she'd brought Forester with her.

But Miracle was striding into the room. She had a fierce look in her eyes, a posture of sheer determination.

But as she drew nearer, her voice lowered, and in a gentle tone, she whispered, "Dearie, it's going to be okay."

Even though she looked as if her expression, her stance had been chiseled from stone, her voice was like a cloud, soft.

She approached her brother, fearlessly. "Honey, it's me. Dearest, please, listen to my voice. It's me."

Dr. Bryant extended a hand, coming closer.

She shot a quick look back at Artemis and her father. Her gaze lingered on Otto for a second longer than made Artemis comfortable, but then her eyes darted away.

Out of the corner of her mouth, she murmured to the two Blythes, "I'm so sorry. I was working late here. If I'd known you were in here, I'd have come sooner."

Artemis hadn't realized the coroner had been given access to the precinct. She hadn't spotted Miracle's flamboyant car in the front parking lot. But then again, oftentimes, coroner's offices had rear entrances, especially if attached to a precinct's main building.

Now, though, Artemis' speculation diminished as she stared at the figure of her brother.

Benjamin looked confused. A dazed expression, his eyes blank.

As he stared at his sister, though, there were cracks in his facade.

Tears were welling up in his eyes now. "Gina," he whispered.

"I know, honey. I know," Bryant said in a coaxing, quiet voice. She approached slowly, extending a hand and cupping her brother's cheek. She left her hand there, smiling up at him. She didn't show an ounce of fear but just cradled her brother's face. "I know dearest. It's so horrible. I am so, so, so sorry."

"She's... she's gone," he whispered. "I... I can't believe she's gone."

He slumped now, his shoulders drooping, his head falling, tears streaming openly down his face.

Bryant leaned in, giving him a big hug, wrapping him in a warm embrace. Artemis and her father stood on the opposite side of the cold, metal table, space between them.

Artemis wasn't sure she'd *ever* been hugged like that.

But Benjamin's only sister kept her arms around him.

He was still shaking.

Artemis swallowed. The last time they'd encountered Dr. Bryant, she'd been reading to one of her old friends in a dreary nursing home.

Something about the woman just seemed drawn to taking care of others.

Artemis felt a strange pang in her own chest as she watched. Her head was throbbing, bruised, and her ego had also taken a beating.

Her father was trying to keep his fake nose in place.

But the two of them just watched as Dr. Bryant held her brother, whispering in his ear.

All the fight, all the fear seemed to leave him now.

He was just crying then clutching at his broken thumb.

There was the sound of footsteps in the hall, now. Hurried steps. The police were finally arriving. Perhaps the desk sergeant had been away from the monitors.

Now, with the sound of Benjamin's crying and the staccato of approaching footsteps, Artemis' mind calmed. If only a little.

She frowned at the brother and sister, and then, quiet enough so only her father could hear, she whispered, "Have you ever seen a hypnosis that strong?"

"Never," he replied. "Not in my life."

She nodded, feeling a faint chill. "I didn't think so. We need to find who did this."

"Of course..." her father was trying to keep his tone even, and though he managed to prevent his voice from shaking, she could hear the fear all the same.

She sighed, then said, "I... I think I have an idea where to start."

"Where?"

"Newlyweds. All of them," she said.

The door banged open. The desk sergeant hurried in. Artemis just watched.

Bryant turned, holding out a hand. "Be gentle. Be gentle!" she pleaded.

The cop slowed, approaching Benjamin's sobbing form. He glanced at Artemis, and she gave a quick nod.

He approached more cautiously.

"His thumb," Artemis said quickly. "It's broken."

The cop nodded and approached, cuffs in hand. All the fight had left Miracle's brother, though, and he didn't put up a fuss.

Artemis just watched, her heart sinking.

Someone had caused all of this. Someone had tampered so horribly with Benjamin Clarkson's mind that he was a shell of himself.

She felt her anger rising.

Her thoughts flitted to Helen.

This was what her sister was like. One moment her sweet, kind, caring self. The next...

Something else took over.

There needed to be a cure for Benjamin. Justice.

Because if she could help him, then she could help Helen.

"What are you thinking?" her father whispered. He ducked his head, glancing away and clearing his throat uncomfortably as he spoke, as Dr. Bryant was looking over in his direction once more, a look of confusion in her eyes.

She didn't recognize Otto, but if anyone could spot him, it was the intelligent coroner.

Artemis could feel her nerves returning. But in a low, quiet voice, watching as the cop cuffed Benjamin, she murmured, "Newlyweds. They're excited, their guards are down... And they often do pre-marital counseling. Who would have better access to create such a mess than a counselor?"

Her father blinked, then nodded once. "It's a good place to start."

She shivered but then turned, sidestepping around the table and moved hastily towards the exit.

CHAPTER 15

"Took you long enough. Where were you?"

Artemis turned to the sound of Forester's voice. The tall agent was standing on the porch of the villa, overlooking the mountain pass. His arms were crossed, and his frown was out in full display.

She grimaced sheepishly and gave an airy wave. "Sorry," she muttered. "Just was out."

Forester sighed. "You know... they *do* call me when something happens, right? Is Dr. Bryant okay?"

Artemis took the stairs with a weary shrug. "Yeah. What time is it?"

"Hour from midnight."

"Wait, really? Shit."

Forester stood on the dark porch, under the canopy of a wooden portico above. He was wearing a plain white t-shirt and pajama bottoms. His hair was even more disheveled than usual.

She found her eyes lingering on his muscled chest, tracing down to where his scar spread along his arm, moving towards the palm of his hand.

Cameron had once been in a fight where his arm had been broken. He'd then knocked the opponent out with his *other* arm. The scar was from the surgery following the fight.

"I need your login info," she said quickly, as she slipped past him into the villa and pulled her laptop from the bag on the lazy-boy chair.

Forester shut the door, following her.

"Why?"

"I need to look something up."

"What?" then, he added. "Just to get the rest out of the way. Who? Where? When?"

"Funny."

She sat down on the chair, resting her laptop on her legs and glancing towards the fire crackling in the fireplace.

She fidgeted uncomfortably, shaking her head and muttering to herself as her fingers flew over the keyboard.

Forester sighed. "I'll type it in."

She was too tired to protest but leaned back. As she did, he moved around behind her, stooped over the armrest, and his arm brushed her shoulder as he typed his credentials into the computer.

The database pulled up, and Artemis stared at the blinking search bar.

As she did, though, she hesitated, feeling where Forester's arm lingered, still resting against her shoulder.

For a moment, the two of them just remained silent, both staring at the computer screen, both listening to the other breathe.

It was late.

Darkness was coming through the windows, spreading like tar across the floor. Artemis could feel her exhaustion consuming her, clouding her thoughts and making her feel drowsy. But the warmth of Forester's arm on her shoulder was doing something else entirely. It was sending a shiver down her spine and making her heart race.

She tried to focus on the task at hand, but her mind kept wandering to the feeling of his touch. She shifted in her seat, trying to get comfortable; she'd already made her choice, hadn't she?

But which one?

Back at the resort, when she'd snuck into his bedroom? Joined him in the shower?

Or after? When she'd realized it had been a mistake.

He didn't even see *her*. He saw someone else. Someone from his past who he'd cared about.

She was little more than a substitute person to him.

"Artemis?" Forester's voice was soft, and she could feel his breath on the back of her neck. "Are you okay?"

She turned to face him, and their eyes met. In the flickering light of the fireplace, she could see the concern mixed with something else.

He leaned back now, as if retreating, or as if frightened he might have startled her.

She sighed softly, closing her eyes, swallowing, and pushing away any further thoughts.

She was alone in a romantic setting with Cameron. No one else to intrude.

Jamie had left.

Her father was staying in a motel at the foot of the mountain.

Her sister and brother were hidden somewhere in Seattle.

It was just the two of them.

But as much as she wanted to think it, she couldn't shake the knowledge of the *others*. Dr. Bryant, for one. Her brother as well.

Suddenly, the warmth along her arm turned cold as her mind conjured up the memory of that interrogation room. She pictured the way Benjamin had reacted to her father's questioning.

The hypnotic effect exerted on him had gone deep.

Someone had tampered with his mind.

She pulled her attention forcefully away from Forester and returned it to the open database. "I just need to find any payments sent by the victims to a marriage counselor. How do I do that?"

"You'll need to contact someone in finance," Forester said. "Or you can use the new app—it works via social security number." He was speaking evenly, acting as if nothing had passed between them. He took another step away from her, though, it seemed to pain him to do so.

She was shaking her head as he retreated. "How do I get the SS, again?"

"Go to the victim's name. Click the hyperlink."

Artemis nodded, refocused completely now as her fingers flew across the keyboard. The latest victim had been a distraction. Just a crime of opportunity attempting to blend in.

But Gina and Sasha? Their husbands had both admitted to the crimes.

They *had* to have someone in common.

Artemis was nibbling on the corner of her lip now, her feet tapping against the floor.

"Is there a way to trace financial transactions by amount?" she said.

Forester frowned. "You're going to need to know this stuff if you want to pass your exam."

"I know, I know," she muttered, waving a hand.

"The only reason Grant was able to get the deal, to get the feds to back off us was if you'd be under her supervision at the field office. To do that, you need to pass the test."

"I get it," she said, more firmly, looking at him now. "I'm not twelve. You don't have to spell it out. *Trust* me, I get it. And it sucks."

Forester just shrugged apologetically. He sighed, looking away now and staring off into the distance, his eyes lingering on the window.

Artemis didn't wait for his instructions, but instead clicked on another tab, cycling through the financial database. Then she began scrolling through the victims' and suspects' financial transactions over the last few months.

It took her a while, line by line, her eyes wanting to glaze, her head wanting to nod. But she knew a lot was counting on her.

Dr. Bryant was counting on her.

Suddenly, her eyes lit up.

"Forester, come look at this," she said, excitement creeping into her voice.

Forester leaned over her shoulder as she pointed to a transaction. "There," she said, "look. Both Sasha and Gina were making similar payments from the accounts directly to this PayWeb account."

Forester nodded, his eyes scanning the screen. "Can you search the PayWeb account? Use quotes for an exact match."

"Right. Ummm... Shit. No..." Artemis frowned, sighing. "It's just the fee for the vineyard."

"No. Hang on. See—there were two payments."

Artemis frowned. "Hmm. What does that mean?"

"Go to the vineyard's website," he said.

She did. Then, he pointed at a white tab on the green heading which read *activities and services.*

She clicked it.

And then scrolled.

"There!" he said quickly. "See that?"

They both went still. Artemis' eyes widened. She was now staring at lettering which read, *Couples Counseling and Marriage Services.*

"The vineyard has a counseling service?" Artemis asked.

Forester shrugged. "Ummm. Looks like it's more of a how-to-spark-the-romance type thing. See? Look at the About section."

"Yeah, I read it. But..." Artemis leaned back, frowning. "Do you think the second payment was for one of the activities? Maybe they were getting connected through the vineyard's own staff."

"Could be... Check to make sure. We need to cross-reference with the other victims' repeated transactions to be sure. See there? Says it should have three installments."

Artemis nodded, her eyes scanning the screen. "I'm on it," she said, her fingers flying across the keyboard once again.

And then she let out a faint breath. "Here! See? Two other payments. Both Gina and Sasha made three payments to the vineyard in addition to their original booking fee."

She could feel her voice rising in excitement and now pushed from the chair, still holding her laptop and cradling it in one arm as she moved back and forth across the floor.

Her eyes zeroed in on the screen. "How come they don't list the names of the counselors on the site?"

"Dunno. Privacy concerns?"

Artemis scowled. "So how do we find out who the couples were speaking with?"

"I mean... I can think of one way."

She turned, glancing at him.

Forester grinned.

Her heart sank. "Wait... you can't be serious."

"Rarely. But this time sorta."

"I'm not going to couples therapy with you, Cameron."

He shrugged. "Suit yourself." He plopped onto a couch and threw his arms behind his head, reclining now and closing his eyes. His muscles were even more pronounced in this posture, through the thin t-shirt. "I just thought you wanted to solve this thing is all."

She glared at him.

He pretended to be sleeping.

She muttered darkly under her breath but then turned to her computer again, bracing it with one arm while her other extended, her fingers moving across the keyboard.

"What are you doing?" he asked, cracking an eye.

"Making a damn appointment. Stop smiling."

CHAPTER 16

Save her... Don't let the wolf get her... SAVE HER!

Javail jolted upright, sitting on patio furniture outside the small, golf-course-facing restaurant.

He blinked a few times, momentarily confused, then reached up and rubbed the sleep from his eyes.

Javail yawned as the morning sunlight streamed across the patio seating. He swirled his glass, causing ice cubes to clink in the confines.

The scent of coffee wafted up from the cold brew, and his fingers were chilled by the condensation slipping along his knuckles.

He sighed, the picture of contentment as he leaned back, studying the features of his new bride.

"You really are something, you know that?" he whispered.

Ayesha smiled sweetly, her cheeks dimpling as she did. Her auburn hair cascaded down her shoulders like a waterfall, and she held his gaze.

The two of them had fallen in love almost instantly, only six months ago. The engagement had been rushed. The wedding even faster.

Some had said they'd eloped, but really they'd just kept the proceedings small—only close family and friends.

And now...

He'd been waiting for some time for this vacation.

"Wine tasting this afternoon?" he said conversationally.

Ayesha nodded but then paused, raising a hand and gesturing at the waiter through the sliding glass doors.

The small restaurant overlooked a golf course behind the vineyard.

The rolling greens and tastefully arranged tree line created a bucolic setting against which to partake in a breakfast of mushroom omelets and fresh grape juice. The grapes came from the vineyard.

The ornate, wooden furniture on the patio was settled under two large, red umbrellas. Another couple was sitting across from them, clinking glasses together in amusement.

A third couple was standing in the doorway, glancing at the tables on the patio as if searching for more seating.

Ayesha looked at him and said, "It's going to kill me."

She was smiling pleasantly.

He blinked. "W-what?"

"I said it's going to kill me. Please stop it!"

He swallowed, blinking and rubbing at his eyes. "Umm..."

"I said did you want coffee?" his wife repeated.

Javail laughed. "Oh. Coffee? I thought you said, er, something else. Sure. I'll have another. Ice please."

His wife was still waving the waitress over.

He shook his head, feeling dizzy now for some reason. He wasn't feeling quite himself.

"Kill it before it kills me..." This time, he heard the words, but his wife's lips hadn't even moved.

He could spend hours studying those lips.

But now, as he stared at the outline of his wife's face, he felt shivers down his spine.

He let out a little breath, picking up the cold coffee and pressing it against his forehead, leaving a streak of icy condensation.

And then...

An image flashed across his mind. A horrible image of a dark, gray creature with yellow eyes.

He let out a little yelp and knocked over his glass. Ice went spilling across the table. And his wife turned to him, startled.

He bounded to his feet, apologizing profusely, and doing his best not to meet the gaze of the other restaurant-goers now glancing in his direction.

He could feel sweat prickling his brow, and his breath came in labored panting.

He knew what he had seen was not just a mere hallucination. He had seen the creature before in his dreams. It was a wolf, a wolf that had been stalking them for days now. He had hoped that a change in venue for breakfast would make it go away, but it seemed to be following him, even here.

Javail took a deep breath, trying to calm his nerves. He glanced around, but the wolf was nowhere to be seen. Maybe it was just a trick of his mind. But he couldn't shake off the feeling of impending danger.

"Are you alright?" Ayesha asked, her hand on his shoulder.

Javail turned to her, still feeling a little disoriented. "Yeah, I'm fine. Just a little clumsy, I guess."

His wife looked at him with concern, but he forced a smile to reassure her. He didn't want to ruin their vacation with his paranoia.

But as they resumed their breakfast, Javail couldn't help but feel a sense of unease. The wolf was still out there, waiting for its chance to attack. He had to be careful. He had to protect his wife, no matter what.

As they finished their meal, Javail's eyes darted around, scanning the surroundings for any sign of danger.

He heard a growl. Coming from under the table.

He yelped again, surging to his feet. His head was starting to spin.

This time, Ayesha stood up as well, a frown etched across her face. "What's wrong, Javail?" she asked, placing a hand on his arm.

He shook his head, trying to shake off the image. "I... I don't know. I just had this..." He noticed the other couple who'd been clinking glasses now watching them curiously.

He dipped his head, frowning. "Nothing. I just... it's the wolf."

"The one from your nightmare?"

"It's not a nightmare," he said, his voice straining, trying to keep as quiet as possible.

Ayesha's brows furrowed. "That's strange," she said softly. "Maybe we should go back to the room and rest for a bit."

Javail nodded, grateful for her understanding.

He quickly snatched the golf cart keys off the table and began to move. His wife went ahead of him, through the glass doors, pulling him beside her. "Just take a second and breathe," she murmured, running her fingers through his hair.

Javail did as he was told, taking deep breaths and trying to calm his racing heart. But the image of the wolf kept flashing across his mind, refusing to let him relax.

And then, suddenly, he felt a sharp pain in his chest. He gasped, clutching at his heart, and Ayesha's eyes widened in alarm.

"Javail, what's happening?" she cried, trying to pull at him.

But the pain had vanished. Panic returned.

"I... I think I need to lie down," he murmured.

His wife's hand felt strange now. As if... as if she had claws digging into his wrist.

He grit his teeth, scowling at the ground and moving quickly, trying to escape the restaurant before it was all too late.

CHAPTER 17

Artemis' foot tapped nervously against the carpet in the counselor's small, lake-facing office.

She hadn't slept well the previous night, filled with anxiety over this particular meeting. She glanced at Forester who was leaning back on the couch, wearing a small smile that refused to vanish from his lips.

He was wearing a bright green, floral shirt and khaki trousers with a mustard stain on the left leg.

He'd noticed the stain while choosing clothing earlier. And had decided to go with the only pair of pants displaying any type of condiment, as if it were a feature rather than a flaw.

Now, though, she settled on one side of the couch in the marriage counselor's office, keeping her distance from her undercover partner.

Both of them were pretending to be married. She hadn't wanted to.

In fact, she'd put up quite a fuss over the issue.

But now, she'd reluctantly given in to Forester's idea.

For all she knew, this was the man hypnotizing the newlyweds.

"Hello," Artemis said, nodding politely as the counselor finally settled in his straight-back, wooden chair.

He smiled at her.

"Thanks for meeting with me on such short notice," the counselor said, beaming brightly. "I don't think I've met you two before. I'm Dr. Grealish."

The man looked like he was in his mid-fifties, with graying hair and creases around his eyes, but his gaze was warm and reassuring.

Artemis nodded, trying to keep her own smile in place.

Grealish folded his hands in his lap, crossing his legs somewhat daintily, his form outlined by the lake view behind him.

He smiled at each of them in turn, and said in a sort of lilting, sing-song voice, "As I'm sure you both know, these sessions aren't quite like what you'd *normally* expect in counseling. Everything here," he spread his arms, indicating the quaint room lined with bookshelves and an oak door, "is designed to get the most out of your relationship with one another. Intimacy is difficult at the *best* of times."

Artemis blinked, certain she'd heard him wrong.

Forester looked suddenly like a child on Christmas morning, leaning forward and waving a hand in a small circle as if to say *go on*.

"The first thing I'd like to ask you both, is what would make today a successful visit for you two? I'm here to help, not to direct. You are in charge of this meeting." He flashed another smile.

He seemed friendly enough. Was it possible he was a killer? Artemis wrinkled her nose. She hadn't wanted to pretend to be Forester's wife just to speak with the counselor, but now she was doubly uncomfortable.

The word *intimacy* was absolutely not something she wanted to discuss with Forester nearby.

Or, for that matter, the stranger in the chair across from her.

"Oh, I'm just here for my wife," Cameron said conversationally.

"Any reason in particular?"

Forester nodded, and the small smirk was still visible. His eyes twinkling. He shot her a mischievous glance, and Artemis went rigid on the couch, one hand gripping the armrest.

She felt the urge, suddenly, to kick him in the leg as he said, "We haven't been enjoying, er, *intimacy* much recently. She's holding out. I don't know why." He shrugged, leaned back, and nodded at the shrink as if giving him permission to do his job.

Dr. Grealish's face shifted into a look of pity. He leaned forward now, his legs still delicately crossed.

171

"I'm sorry to hear there have been issues. Sometimes, when in a new place, sleeping in a new bed, it can just take some time to get used to things."

"Oh, it's not just here," Forester said before Artemis could redirect the conversation. "We haven't slept together in... what was it, honey—weeks, now? The last time was at a resort."

"A resort? I see. Do you two often go on holiday together back to back?"

Forester gave a little sniff. "You know, just trying to keep things fresh. But I just..." He gave another, more exaggerated sniff, running a finger under his eye. "I just don't think she finds me attractive anymore. It's the stretch marks, I bet. I shouldn't have hit the gym so much!"

The counselor tisked his tongue. "Oh, dear. Oh, dear. It's really that serious, then, is it? What do you say, Andi? Is there something in what your husband is mentioning you'd like to address?"

Artemis crossed her arms, scowling at Cameron. "No."

The counselor didn't reply, waiting patiently for her to continue.

She didn't want to. Forester was poking fun, and they were here for reconnaissance alone. But as she thought about it, she realized it wasn't such a bad play to find out how Dr. Grealish would treat them if he found a vulnerability.

That was the theory, wasn't it? Someone was targeting the emotionally vulnerable at their weakest?

She frowned, biting her lip and feeling a flare of pain in order to shock herself to her senses.

"How often do you two sleep with each other in a given week?" the therapist said, crossing his legs in the opposite direction this time. He spoke earnestly and leaned forward as if he were all ears.

"Five or six times a week, usually," Forester said.

"Rarely. Almost never," Artemis shot back. She scowled.

"That shower play-time wasn't *never*," Forester retorted.

"You're insufferable."

"Whoa, whoa, Andi. No need to call names. I'm sure your husband wants to hear your heart." Dr. Grealish flashed another, sincere smile.

"Why don't you two turn, face each other, and hold one another's hands."

Before Artemis could refuse, Forester had turned fully, extending both hands and looking her directly in the eyes.

She wanted to punch him on the nose.

But they had a witness... So, with a scowl at him, she turned slowly, readjusting on the couch, and extended her own arms, hands up.

Dr. Grealish watched them closely, his expression still warm and friendly. "Now, I want you both to take a deep breath and look into each other's eyes. Really see each other."

Artemis rolled her eyes but complied, taking a deep breath and meeting Forester's gaze. She saw the amusement in his eyes but also a hint of something else, something she couldn't quite put her finger on.

"Good," Dr. Grealish said, his voice soothing. "Now, I want you both to say one thing you appreciate about each other."

Artemis hesitated, her mind going blank. She couldn't think of anything she appreciated about Forester at the moment.

But then he spoke up, his voice surprisingly sincere. "I appreciate how dedicated Andi is to her family. She's one of the most loyal people I've ever met."

Artemis was taken aback. She stared at him, studying his face. He was a handsome man. She'd always known it. But now, sitting this close, looking him in the eye, she spotted the weariness as well.

Some of the humor seemed to have drained from his features now as he looked at her.

He swallowed briefly, his brow dipping for a moment.

His hands were warm to the touch. And she could feel Grealish watching them both.

Perhaps even watching them a bit *too* closely.

Out of the corner of her eye, she felt him lean forward even further, hands pressed against his knees.

"And you, Andi? What's something you appreciate about your husband?"

His tone had also changed now, too. A bit breathier, as if he were exhaling and inhaling through his mouth alone.

He wasn't blinking as he stared at them.

She didn't look directly towards him, though, and instead, still meeting Forester's gaze, she said, "I appreciate how good you are at blending in. You make it look effortless."

Dr. Grealish nodded, his smile widening. "That's a great start." But then he paused. "Umm... hang on. What do you mean *blending* in?"

Artemis released her grip on Cameron, pulling away and pinching his arm fiercely as she did.

He gave a satisfying little jolt as she looked at Grealish now.

"Oh, you know—he's a social butterfly. He really knows how to blend into social situations."

"Ah, I see," said the counselor. "Hmm... Well, doesn't that feel better now? The two of you *both* know something the other appreciates."

Forester was nodding sincerely. "I really appreciate it, doc," he said.

Artemis, though, cleared her throat and cut in. "Actually... I was wondering if there's some *other* method we might be able to use. Something a bit more *stringent.*"

He smiled benignly at her. "Whatever do you mean?" Grealish asked.

This was the tricky part. Artemis' mouth felt dry. She knew she couldn't spook him. If he thought, for whatever reason, she was playing with him, the conversation would end sooner than it had started.

Hell, she might easily be putting them both in harm's way.

But on the other hand, if she *didn't* press a bit, it might take weeks for him to reveal anything.

Nothing ventured, nothing gained.

She thought of Dr. Bryant. Of the two poor victims.

And so she said, "We had some friends who highly recommended you, actually."

He suddenly brightened at this. The counselor smoothed back some of his silver hair, his wrinkles more pronounced in the corners of his eyes as he smiled.

"Really? What a treat. No, I mean it. What a *real* treat. Ha! That makes my day. No, my *week.*" He clicked his fingers as if giving silent applause to himself.

His legs crossed and uncrossed again, this time right over left.

Artemis said, "But one thing they mentioned was that you were *very* good at non-traditional modes of counseling."

She paused, raising an eyebrow significantly. She didn't want to come out and say the word *hypnosis*. That would undoubtedly spook the man.

No... She needed to play it slow. To reel him in.

He looked puzzled, briefly, and was leaning back now. A defensive posture? Was he now guarded?

Or was he just confused?

He said, puzzled, "I'm not sure what you mean by non-traditional modes of counseling."

Artemis bit her lip, considering how to proceed. She knew she had to tread carefully, but at the same time, she had to push him to reveal more.

"Well, our friends said that you had some unique techniques that you used with your patients. Techniques that were... unconventional, shall we say?"

Dr. Grealish's expression was guarded now, his eyes narrowed as if he were studying her. "I'm not sure what you're getting at," he said slowly.

Artemis took a deep breath, steeling herself. She watched as Grealish's face paled slightly, his eyes darting back and forth between her and Forester. He seemed to be weighing his options, trying to decide how much to reveal.

"Is it true?" she pressed.

Grealish hesitated for a moment, then nodded slowly. "Yes, I do use… unique techniques in some cases. But only with the patient's full consent, of course."

Artemis nodded, trying to keep her expression neutral.

"Do you mind showing us?" Forester asked, and he had gone tense on the couch next to her.

Grealish looked extremely uncomfortable now. He bit his lower lip, glanced past them towards the door, but then stood to his feet.

"One moment. I'll get what we need. Just sit right there."

And then, before anyone could protest, he hastened through a door in the back of the office, off into a side room. The door shut behind him with a *thud,* leaving Artemis and Forester alone in the would-be murderer's office.

CHAPTER 18

Dr. Grealish returned a few minutes later, carrying a suspicious, black tote bag.

Artemis leaned back, uncomfortably, her shoulder blades pressed against the cushioned backrest.

At her side, on the couch in the psychologist's office, Forester still looked the picture of contentment, like a lazy tom cat sprawled in a sunbeam.

And now, the sun was coming through the window facing the vineyard.

The mountains in the distance attempted to block the sun with sheer, gray cliffs and slopes of green foliage.

The scenic view, however, didn't capture Artemis' gaze the way the black zipper bag in Grealish's hand did.

The nervous counselor locked the door behind him with an ominous *click* then turned to face the two of them.

He shifted nervously from foot to foot, a faint tinge creeping across his features.

Artemis' heart was pounding.

Was this the man who'd hypnotized the murderers? Was he the one who'd been tampering with Benjamin Clarkson's mind?

Artemis waited now, just watching, attentive. Her suspicions arose, and prickles erupted across her skin, causing her hands to bunch into fists in her lap.

Was he going to try and hurt them?

Grealish slowly unzipped his bag, his features turning red. He shook his head side to side, stammering, "I don't normally... you know. With strangers. Just..." He flashed a quick, schoolboy grin that didn't fit his aged features. "You know. If you come with references."

Then, he began to pull items from inside the bag. Artemis blinked, stared, and then her jaw unhinged.

Forester let out a burst of laughter, throwing back his head.

Grealish, holding onto what looked like a leather whip, went still.

He stared at the two of them, and then the red flush along his face completely took over. He scowled and hastily stowed his whip and assortment of toys. He quickly zipped the bag up, stammering, scowling.

"You come here just to mock me?" he snapped.

Artemis could feel her own face warming up now. Forester, though, was still chuckling, shaking his head side to side.

The tall man pushed to his feet now, pointing at the bag. "You mean to say *that* is your version of special counseling?"

Grealish scowled. "I thought you said you knew?"

Forester shook his head side to side. Artemis was still flushed, and she moved away from the couch.

Her mind was racing, and slowly, she pieced it all together. She stared at the counselor, her eyes wide, and then she stammered, "You mean to say that you try to sleep with your clients?"

He blinked, paused, then slowly lowered his bag of toys behind a desk. Now, he looked like a chastised child, hanging his head, shoulders slumped.

"It's just some harmless fun. Some of the clients think it helps them loosen up."

Artemis shot Forester a horrified look, but the fighter was just shaking side to side.

"You randy bastard," Forester said, but it was with a good-natured tone. "How many? Just for my own curiosity?"

"What?"

"How many of your couples agree to... special sessions?"

Grealish scowled. "Normally, I feel it out first."

"Oh, I bet you do."

"That's not what I meant!"

"So how many?"

"Not many. Just those who show a willingness. This is a romantic place, *sir*. A non-judgmental space, I might add. You two could learn a thing or two in your relationship." He paused, then glanced towards Artemis and back to Forester. "Are you sure you both don't want to—"

"We're sure," Artemis snapped.

Forester was still grinning.

But Artemis wasn't ready to leave just yet. Perhaps he was playing them for a fool. Just because he had a bag of adult toys and a sheepish disposition didn't mean he wasn't their psychopathic hypnotist.

She glanced around the office space, now, scowling. And then, she said, "Do you know Benjamin Clarkson?"

He blinked. "Who?"

"Benjamin Clarkson?"

"I... I can't say that I do."

Artemis frowned. "How come he was paying you for sessions then?"

Grealish just shook his head, standing stiff and tall, as if an iron rod were installed in his spine. He said, "I don't take payments personally. Whatever do you mean?"

"We saw the payments in his account," Artemis said firmly.

Now, Grealish's eyes narrowed. "Are you... are you law enforcement?" Suddenly he froze. The pieces fell into place, and his mouth unhinged. "This is about those deaths, isn't it!" he said in a low whisper. And then, the rest of the realization struck, and his hand darted up to his chest, pressing to his shirt. "You don't think I had anything to do with it, do you?" he yelled.

Artemis just frowned. "Why was Clarkson paying your office money?"

"I'm not the only counselor who works here!" he yelled. "We have seven on staff."

"I checked already," Artemis retorted. "Three are at a separate location. Two are currently on vacation. And besides you, the only other counselor is in a wheelchair. I checked the surgical records."

He stared at her, stunned now as she rattled it all off. Part of her felt a small, vindictive pleasure at taking him off guard in the way that he'd done with her.

Grealish's eyes darted around the room, looking for an escape. "I don't know what you want from me," he muttered, his voice shaking with fear. "I'm just a counselor. I help people."

Artemis leaned forward, her eyes locked on his. "Then help us," she said firmly. "Help us find out who is behind these murders."

Grealish swallowed hard, his eyes flickering with fear. "I don't know anything," he whispered. "I swear."

Artemis leaned back, her eyes still locked on his. He seemed genuine in his fear. He was a horny old man who took advantage of his clients, but that didn't mean he was a killer.

Suddenly, he exclaimed, "Look! Look. My client list. I can show you—it's assigned by the vineyard office, so I can't change it. Look!"

He was now hastening to a desk, grabbing his laptop, and turning it so she could see.

He clicked a couple of times then jammed the computer towards her. "See!" he exclaimed. "No Clarkson. That's a full client list. Believe it or not," he said, with an air of wounded dignity, "I'm somewhat popular with the resort guests."

"I bet," Forester snickered.

But Artemis was frowning, reading through the list. She said, slowly, "Maybe you removed Clarkson's name."

"I can't. See? It's a locked file. It's sent by the office. Look at the email date—there's no way I could've altered that. It's the original client list. No Clarkson!" Now, he looked relieved, as if he'd just laid down a trump card.

But then, her eyes landed on another name. Ramirez, Leo.

She frowned. "What about him?" she asked.

He blinked, leaned in. And then he froze. "Oh shit... Ramirez... That was the name in the paper."

"So you did know him?"

"We only ever met once!" exclaimed Grealish, his voice rising an octave. "I swear. See? Look. It was three weeks ago. We met once and..." Grealish hesitated, then stammered, "And I propositioned him and his wife, but he was creeped out and said they weren't coming back. That was it. I swear."

Forester was no longer chuckling now. "So you did know one of our victims," he said.

"Only briefly. For a half-hour session. That was it. Then he left."

Artemis looked back at the schedule again. Indeed, there were no other appointments for the Ramirez's. No sign of the Clarksons.

Which meant the families must have visited different counselors.

What if the counseling angle was all wrong?

Artemis paused, then said, on a sudden hunch, "Did Ramirez mention any other counselors? Was he seeing anyone else?"

"I... I don't..."

But then, Grealish went suddenly still.

"What?"

"Umm..." A swallow. "I'm sure it's nothing. I just remember how he, and look, I only remember this because of how odd it was."

"What did he say?"

"He said that their group sessions were far more professional."

Artemis blinked. "Group?"

"Yeah. That's what he said. I just remember because he'd gotten... you know... mad. Believe it or not," Grealish sniffed, "I'm not turned down that frequently."

Artemis was shaking her head now, glancing at Forester as if looking for some further lead.

The tall agent shrugged, though.

Artemis bit her lip.

She knew they had to find out more about these group sessions. It was a lead they couldn't ignore. But where to start?

Then, an idea struck her. "Can you access the resort's database?" she asked Grealish.

He nodded, still looking uneasy.

"Pull up any information on group counseling sessions," she said. "We need to know who is running them and when they're held."

Grealish hesitated but then started typing away on his laptop. He pulled up a list of all the counseling sessions held at the resort but then shook his head. "See? Nothing. We don't do groups. This is a couples retreat."

"Some of you do groups," Forester muttered.

"But not like *that*!" he snapped back.

Artemis scanned the list, looking for any familiar names, but nothing jumped out at her.

There were a few wine-tasting tours, a light show, and more than one movie romantic movie night.

But nothing to do with a group session.

Artemis frowned now. What if the resort counselors were a red herring? What if this group he'd mentioned was where they should be looking?

Grealish didn't seem guilty.

The schedule that displayed Clarkson wasn't on his list. In addition, his embarrassment had seemed genuine.

She didn't linger to watch him, and instead, she turned and headed towards the door, Forester right behind her. As she opened the door, she turned back to Grealish. "Oh, and one more thing," she said, her eyes narrowing. "If we find out that you've been playing games with your clients again, we'll be back. And this time, we won't be so nice."

And with that, she turned and walked out of the room, leaving Grealish standing there, his face drained of all color.

As they moved into the hall, Forester said, "I'll have someone tap his phone. Just to keep an eye on him."

"It's not him," she said as soon as they were far enough down the hall that he couldn't overhear.

"You're sure?"

"Pretty damn sure. He's too timid. Not the type. Plus the schedule didn't list Clarkson."

"Maybe he changed it. Could've been lying. Emails are hard to fake but not impossible."

She nodded. "Good to keep an eye on him then, but we've got nothing on him. We can check with the office to see if Clarkson really was assigned to a different therapist."

"Yeah, good call. Then?"

"Then... we need to see what group Leo was talking about."

The two of them emerged from the counselor's office, walking quickly. As they left, though, Artemis' attention was redirected by a small restaurant with patio seating built alongside the office wall.

The main building served as a welcome center with smaller structures built off a central hub, overlooking the vineyard.

And now, as they emerged from the counselor's wing, a sudden commotion broke out from the patio seating.

Then someone screamed.

CHAPTER 19

It took Artemis a split-second to realize the source of the scream.

Figures were scrambling over toppled furniture. Plates of food were knocked off the edge of the table as figures scampered back.

Artemis stared, wide-eyed, her gaze quickly drawn to a man.

He was crying, a butter knife clutched in one hand. He brandished it, waving it at the other restaurant-goers.

His other hand, though, tightened around the wrist of a sobbing woman.

"Don't! Honey, please! What are you doing?"

He was dragging her towards the railing. The patio seating was on the second floor, overlooking a twelve-foot drop.

The man with the butterknife had a glaze-eyed look as he muttered beneath his breath, "Don't hurt her. Please don't..."

He dragged her along at his side.

The woman was crying now, tears streaking her features. Her voice tremored as she pleaded with the man. "Don't do it! Honey—honey, listen! There's no wolf! You're hurting me."

It was the word *wolf* that jarred Forester into action.

He bolted like a sprinter at the sound of a starter pistol, racing forward and flinging himself up a tasteful, wooden trellis leading up to the patio.

Artemis broke into a sprint as well. She watched as Forester climbed the railing.

She didn't expect to be able to do the same, so she hastened towards the stairs leading up from the garden path to the restaurant seating.

She reached the patio a second after Forester. Both were breathing heavily.

It was Forester, though, who'd spread a hand in front of him like a traffic warden. His other hand gripped his firearm, which he pointed off to the side.

"Let her go!" Forester demanded.

The man stared at him, eyes vacant. He still clutched the butter knife but shook his head, yanking the woman's arm once more. Forester aimed.

"Don't!" the woman screamed. "Please don't! Javail! Dammit, listen!"

"Ma'am, what's going on?" Artemis called out, her voice tense.

"My husband. He's—my arm! Stop, Javail, stop!"

Artemis was at Forester's side, she muttered under her breath, "He's hypnotized. Just like the others."

The rest of the restaurant-goers had retreated to a safe distance, gawking from within the glass sliding doors.

The breeze picked up, sweeping across the patio, and Artemis felt her skin prickle with the chill.

Forester didn't take his eyes off the man, his grip on the firearm tightening. "He's going to throw her over the railing..."

Artemis didn't answer, instead taking a step forward, her hands raised in a placating gesture. "Javail, please. You don't want to hurt your wife."

The man shook his head, his grip on the knife unyielding. He had dark hair to match dark eyes and sharp, handsome features arranged in a puzzled look. "I have to. The wolf, it's coming. It's coming for us all."

Artemis exchanged a worried glance with Forester before taking another step forward. "Javail, there's no wolf. We can help you."

Javail's eyes flickered to Artemis, his gaze piercing. "You can't help me. Nobody can. It's too late."

Artemis took another step, her heart pounding. "It's not too late. You just need to let your wife go, and we can take you somewhere safe."

Javail's grip on his wife's arm tightened, and she whimpered in pain. "I can't. It's too dangerous. You don't understand."

Artemis took another step, her breath coming in quick pants. Forester was angling off to the side. She could feel him training his gun past her.

If he thought he had to, he wouldn't hesitate to shoot.

Now, her skin prickled, and her tongue felt like wool in her mouth.

"Javail," she whispered. "I can help you with the wolf. Would you like that?"

Partnering in one's delusion was rarely advised. But right now, either Forester shot the man dead, or he flung his wife head first onto hard asphalt.

Neither eventuality was appealing.

She kept her hands splayed in front of her, both extended as if attempting to hold back some unseen force.

She focused on her tone, keeping it calm. She focused on her breathing, attempting to match his.

Without the anchor phrase, the keyword, she wouldn't be able to undo what had been done.

But personal knowledge could help.

Forming a connection, redirecting neural pathways could help focus someone's mind.

She didn't know much about this man.

But she did have a guess.

Something Grealish had said about Ramirez.

"How are the group meetings going?" she said quickly, hoping that the combination of the question and the surprise of the knowledge would capture his attention.

He blinked, surprised.

She felt a thrill of exhilaration. Recognition had dawned in his eyes.

"Yeah," she said quietly. "A group. I know about it. Do you remember what sort of group it was?"

"Of course," he snapped. And for a moment, his gaze looked coherent.

His wife was still trying to pry at his fingers while simultaneously stroking his arm in a comforting gesture. "It's going to be okay. Please, honey. It's okay."

Artemis noticed the placations and noticed the way it seemed to raise Javail's ire. The more his wife spoke, the more his eyes seemed to widen in fear.

He looked at her, froze, and then seemed to panic. "No, no, no," he moaned.

He pushed her against the rail. She yelled, her voice piercing the air. She nearly toppled, her hair cascading over the rail, her head tilting towards the asphalt below, but she'd managed to snatch a handful of his shirt, holding on for dear life.

Artemis had stepped to the side, blocking Forester's line of sight.

She didn't want this man dead.

She couldn't allow it.

It's not absolution for doubting your father... a small, nasty voice whispered in her mind.

But she ignored it, pushing the thought aside. "Please don't talk," she said quickly to the wife. "Your voice. Something in your voice is triggering the fear. Trust me. Please!"

The woman was still whimpering, still holding onto her husband's shirt, tightly.

Artemis took another step forward, her voice still soothing, her posture small, hunched in on itself. Presenting that she wasn't a threat.

"Javail," she said, "Just listen to my voice. Alright? Listen to me."

The man's wife looked like she wanted to say something again, but Artemis gave her a firm look, shaking her head quickly.

As time passed since the woman's last outburst, Javail looked a bit more clear-eyed.

Something about his wife's voice... And then Artemis realized. The voice was the anchor. Or at least, part of it.

That was why it had been nearly impossible to get the other two men to let their guards down. The hypnosis had been grounded in their wives' voices. And when their wives had died, so had the source to release the spell cast over them.

Now, though, Artemis could feel her own fear rising.

Just because she knew the anchor, didn't mean she knew how to trigger it.

From what she could tell, whenever Javail's wife spoke, it only irritated him further. Made him scared.

Scared of what?

"No one's going to hurt her!" Artemis called out suddenly. "Please, listen. She's safe. Your wife is safe. She's fine."

"She's not!" he yelled.

"Okay. Okay, but I'm here to help you save her. Is that the wolf? In your hand? Do you have the wolf?"

He looked at his wife, eyes wide with fear. "Yes," he moaned.

His wife was crying now.

Artemis nodded, her fears confirmed. The hypnosis was creating a monster in the man's own subconscious. But his mind was tricking him into thinking his wife was the threat.

A sick, twisted trick by whoever had done this.

But Artemis was determined that everyone would make it off the patio alive.

So she lied. "I'm a wolf-tamer. I came here to train the wolf. Can I do that? Please?"

He was staring at her, eyes bleary, unable to see clearly. His wife was still crying.

"Trust me. This is the only way to help your wife," Artemis said. "You must really love her. To face a wolf with your bare hands. You must *really* love her."

He nodded fiercely.

Artemis stepped forward again.

But he tensed once more.

She had a split second to act.

Normally, Forester was the type to engage with threats physically. She would stay back, keeping her distance.

But now...

She was the one within striking distance.

She didn't want to hurt him. Just to help him.

Forester had been training her over the intervening weeks, in preparation for the field test.

And now... though her anxiety was swirling and her stomach was tight, she knew she had to *act*.

So she did.

It took all her courage, but standing two paces away, she suddenly lunged in.

Her hand snapped out, thumb out, knuckles tensed, throwing with her arm, following through, just like Forester had taught.

She struck him on the wrist as he howled in horror.

His fingers uncurled, briefly.

Javail's grip on his wife's arm loosened, and she took the opportunity to slip out of his grasp. She stumbled backwards, her eyes wide with fear.

Artemis stepped in, blocking Javail from pursuing her. She wrapped both arms around him, holding him back as he tried to charge past her. She kept her voice soft and soothing. "It's okay," she whispered desperately into his ear. "Everything is going to be okay."

Javail struggled a bit more, but now Forester was at his side, gripping his shoulder.

Cameron shot Artemis a quick look, nodding as if impressed.

Javail quailed under Forester's massive grip; his eyes flickered between Artemis and his wife, his expression contorted in confusion. "What's happening?"

"You're under hypnosis," Artemis said gently. "But it's okay. We can help you. We just need you to come with us."

Javail shook his head, his eyes darting around wildly. "I can't leave. The wolf is coming. It's going to kill us all."

Artemis took a step forward, her heart pounding in her chest. "There's no wolf," she said firmly. "It's just a delusion. We can help you break free from it."

Javail's expression softened slightly, and he took a step towards her. "You can help me?"

Artemis nodded, her eyes locked on his. "Yes," she said. "We can help you."

Javail looked down at his hands, his expression troubled. "You have to help her. Before it's too late."

Artemis nodded gently, releasing her grip on him. Forester began to guide Javail away. His wife continued to cry, sobbing horribly...

Worst of all, though, the man couldn't even seem to hear her tears.

His eyes were blank. And whenever he looked in the direction of the love of his life, he just looked terrified.

He was seeing a wolf.

What did any of it mean?

Artemis shared another look with Forester, this one much more grim, as the two of them hastened down the wooden stairs, back to the parking lot, leading their would-be wolf-killer ahead of them.

CHAPTER 20

The counselor moved slowly through the trees, hands behind his back, a small smile affixed to his lips.

He was in a good mood.

The sunlight had lifted on the horizon, sending streaks of light across the horizon. In the distance, he spotted the mountains, jutting up like sentries against the sky.

The sun warmed his skin, and he listened to the faint panting of his companion at his side.

A huffing, hungry sound coming from the wolf.

He leaned down, scratching the creature behind the ears, feeling the coarse fur and the frail cartilage of ear tissue.

His hand moved down to the wolf's neck, still scratching. He felt the thrum of the heartbeat. He wondered what would happen if he squeezed.

The wolf was powerful, yes... But it was in his thrall, under his control.

He continued strolling along the path. In the distance, he could hear laughter, people at play. He strolled past a small park with plastic play sets where children were climbing on pink monkey bars or sliding down bright blue slides.

He gave a little wave to one of the mothers sitting on a park bench.

She stared back at him, looking suddenly uneasy. Her eyes kept darting to his animal.

He'd never named the wolf.

It seemed a cruel thing to name a wolf.

And while he wasn't averse to cruelty, he had a particular code where this sort of thing was involved.

The woman's fear aroused something in him, so he stopped, staring at her.

She was on her feet now, nervously waving over a small, six-year-old blonde boy. The boy was busy digging in the sand and ignored his mother.

Just the presence of the wolf was frightening her.

So the counselor remained affixed to the spot, staring towards the playset, openly leering at the woman.

He didn't keep moving but, rather, allowed his presence to intimidate.

She was now trying to gather her son in her arms, to carry him back to the park bench. "That's enough for today," the woman was saying hurriedly.

The counselor just watched.

Fear in a woman's eyes was a delectable thing.

He considered the last time a woman had been frightened in his presence, and his lips twisted into a snarl. Stupid whore. She'd gotten what was coming to her after all those years.

He felt a lance of embarrassment as memories collided with the present.

He shook his head as if to dislodge cobwebs.

"Nice puppy."

He looked up suddenly.

A small child, no older than five, was staring at the wolf, having abandoned a red bucket in the sand, and now approached.

There were only four children playing on the park set, and only two women within sight corralling them. The one who'd initially spotted him was still struggling to entice her son away from the diggers in the dirt.

Now, though, the counselor peered down his nose at the small child.

The little one was reaching out with splayed fingers, sticky from some mid-morning snack.

"Is it nice?" the child said, wrinkling his nose.

The counselor stared down at him. He wondered what might happen if he let the young one pet the wolf. Dark and pleasing images flashed through his mind.

The women on those benches would certainly caterwaul then. He chuckled now.

"Oh, he's very friendly," the counselor said.

The young boy wrinkled his nose but then reached out, patting the wolf on the ears.

The creature immediately began to growl, lips pulling back, teeth showing.

The counselor's smile widened as he watched the child's hand go limp, the sticky fingers slipping from the wolf's fur. The beast's growls grew louder, more threatening, and the counselor reveled in the fear emanating from the small child.

Another mother on a bench was now on her feet, shouting for her child to come back to them. The counselor held up a hand, motioning for them to stay where they were.

The wolf continued to growl, eyes locked on the child. The counselor reached down, grabbing the child by the arm and pulling him closer to the beast.

"Watch," he said, his voice low and menacing.

The child began to cry, trying to pull his arm back. The counselor held on a moment longer. But the woman was now running towards him.

No sense in giving her a long look at his face up close.

He didn't need the trouble.

He had other plans for today.

So he released the boy, gave him a little push, then turned, moving back up the path and leading the wolf.

Today was going to be a very big day.

CHAPTER 21

Artemis strode back and forth, her hands in her pockets, her eyes fixated on the man across from her.

Forester watched from hooded eyes, standing by the door with his arms crossed.

Javail was shivering now, his teeth biting his lower lip. His eyes were bloodshot, and he kept twitching, looking about the room as if searching for his favorite fix. She'd seen people struggling with drug addiction behave similarly.

No one spoke at first, but then Javail said, "How long until he gets here? Is he really going to be able to help me?"

Artemis flinched but nodded. She could feel Forester watching her closely.

Her father was on the way.

She'd texted his burner phone, and he'd agreed to come, wearing his disguise.

It was a testament to his desire to mend fences with his daughter that he wasn't refusing an audience in the presence of an FBI agent.

Forester was a friend. A trusted confidant, but also... she doubted his loyalty would go as far as aiding and abetting the Ghost Killer.

The FBI still believed her father was the guilty one.

He'd kept the secret in prison about his daughter, protecting Helen.

And now the master hypnotist was on his way to help his youngest child crack the case.

She tried not to look at Forester, her nerves rising. Would he recognize Otto, despite the prosthetics? Forester had sat down across from her father in the past. At the time, Otto had brought up something about Forester's own past, as if reading his mind.

She was beginning to think this was a bad idea.

But before her feet became too cold, there was a quiet tapping sound on the door.

Forester stepped back, opening the metal door and allowing a squint-eyed man with a paunch to enter the room.

Her father's disguise was even more pronounced than last time. His wispy hair was combed back, and he wore a two-piece suit. His eyes kept roaming around the room, and his limp slowed his progress into the space.

Artemis chewed nervously on her lip, shooting glances to Forester to see if he could see through her father's disguise.

For the moment, though, the tall fed was still watching Javail.

Their would-be killer was still twitching and fidgeting like a junkie in search of a needle.

At last, he called out, his voice shrill as if he were in pain. "Is this the guy who's going to help me?"

Artemis began to nod, but before she could, her father stepped in front of the metal table and tapped his hand against the surface with a staccato sound that resounded in the room.

Knuckles against metal made a tolling noise like a bell, and Javail suddenly perked up.

Her father spoke. "It's a pleasure to meet you, sir."

He did so with a high-tempo, energetic voice. Some, in the mentalism world, called it *turning up the brightness.* Taking a separate stance from a normal, slow cadence that came with the hypnotist's anchoring phrase.

Her father continued to speak quickly.

Forester was now watching both men, his expression curious.

Artemis had told him that it was an old family friend who could help.

He'd trusted her enough not to question deeper.

And now, they watched as Otto said, "Don't think, just tell me: how long has this been going on?"

Javail hesitated, biting his lower lip.

Artemis could see the fear in Javail's eyes, but she knew her father was skilled at getting people to open up. She watched as he continued to speak, his voice still high-tempo and energetic.

"Come on, you can tell me. How long have you been seeing the ghost?"

Javail's eyes widened, his whole body shaking. "I don't know what you're talking about. I haven't seen any ghosts."

Artemis watched as her father leaned in closer to Javail, his eyes locked onto his.

"You have to trust me," he said, his voice dropping to a low whisper. "I'm here to help you. But I need you to be honest with me. How long have you been seeing the ghost?"

Javail hesitated for a moment longer; Artemis watched as her father's eyes locked onto his, his fingers tapping against the metal table. She felt a moment of confusion, but then she realized what her father was doing.

Establishing a secondary anchoring phrase. *Ghost. Ghost.*

Giving him something to fear besides a wolf.

Her father's posture mirrored Javail's. His cadence kept time with the way Javail's eyes flicked back and forth.

Everything in cohesion.

It was like watching a master at work. Her father had always been skilled at getting people off guard, to reveal their deepest fears and secrets. And as Javail continued to speak, his voice growing more and more frantic, Artemis could see that he was finally beginning to break. "I never saw a ghost! I never did! It's a damn wolf. It's trying to eat my wife!"

"There is no wolf!" her father snapped, his voice harsh and resonate. "Tell me that. Say it now. No. Don't think. Tell me there is no wolf!"

She watched as her father leaned in again, this time making physical contact, gripping Javail's wrist tight. "It's a ghost. Not a wolf."

Forester looked at the spectacle with some degree of skepticism, his eyebrow high on his forehead.

But Artemis knew that while it looked silly, the subconscious could be an unpredictable place.

Her father tapped his knuckles against the table again, leaning in and meeting the young man's gaze.

"Remember the ghost?" Now, her father's voice had switched to a calmer, more soothing tone. His hand gripped Javail's shoulder. "The ghost is near. The ghost, right?"

Javail shuddered as her father's grip tightened. His eyes were wide with fear, the whites showing around his irises. "It's a ghost," he repeated, his voice shaking. "Not a wolf."

Her father nodded, releasing his grip on Javail's wrist. "Good, good," he said, his voice returning to its high-tempo, energetic tone. "Now, tell me everything you can about this ghost. What does it look like? Where does it appear?"

Javail took a deep breath, his body still shaking. "It's a man," he said, his voice barely above a whisper. "He's pale, with long hair. He appears in the living room every night at midnight."

Artemis felt a chill run down her spine.

Her father nodded thoughtfully. "And what does he do?"

"He just stands there, watching me," Javail said, his voice growing more frantic. "And then he disappears."

Her father leaned back, his fingers steepled together. "Interesting," he said. "And this ghost... is anything else in the scene with it?"

Javail blinked. "What ghost?"

"The ghost you told me about. The ghost who might endanger the woman you love."

"There's... next to the ghost. A wolf!" he suddenly yelled. "There's a wolf!"

He toppled back, the chair nearly hitting the floor, but Forester had noticed the momentum and lunged forward, snatching the chair and preventing it from falling.

Now Javail was sobbing, his voice shaking as he shook his head side to side.

He trembled, and once again looked jittery.

Artemis watched her father, frowning.

He turned to her, his deep brow furrowing. She noticed a piece of prosthetic adhesive trailing from his nose.

She resisted the urge to reach out and remove it.

Instead, as Forester helped Javail settle back in his seat again, she whispered, "What's that about a ghost?"

Her father said, "The source of the fear. The real threat. I needed to give him something indirect to project onto."

"So... you think this hypnotist is a man with long hair?"

"A pale man with long hair, yes."

"You're sure?"

"No. But I think it's a good guess. Another thing..."

"Yeah?"

Her father shot a look towards where Javail was now sobbing on the table. Her father's features twisted into something of a sympathetic glance but then returned to look at her.

He said, "The wolf showed up with the ghost."

"So?"

"I think it's real."

"The wolf is? How?"

"It was concrete even in a projection. It causes this much fear. I think whoever did this to them has a real-life wolf."

Artemis blinked, then murmured, "Are you sure?"

Again, she could've predicted the answer. "No."

She sighed, turning away from him and then saying, "Can you spend a few minutes with him? Maybe try to get him to calm down? I promised you'd help him."

Her father glanced back at the suspect, then nodded. "I can see what I can do. But... We need privacy."

Artemis hesitated, meeting her father's gaze.

"You have to trust me," he said in a low murmur. "I think I've earned some leeway."

She felt uncomfortable now but nodded. "Alright. Fine. I need to speak with Cameron out in the hall anyway."

"Cameron?" her father said, his eyebrows inching up.

"It's just a name," she muttered, unsure what he was implying.

She hastened away now, moving towards the door and gesturing at Forester.

The ex-fighter followed her into the hall and only spoke once the door had closed behind them.

A faint hum came from a vending machine off to their left, and the blue glow illuminated the corridor.

"What happened?" Forester said.

"He thinks the killer owns a wolf. A real wolf."

"Seriously?"

"Yeah."

"Not a very common thing to own. But there are wolves in Washington state. Need permits, though. Can't own one as a pet. Municipal public safety law."

She stared at him.

"What? I looked into it a few years ago. Wanted a crocodile." He grinned.

"Sure you did." She shook her head and resisted the urge to roll her eyes. Instead, she crossed her arms and turned away from the glowing vending machine.

Through the window of the interrogation room, she spotted her father sitting across the table from Javail.

"This family friend of yours seems to know what he's doing," Forester said.

"Umm, yeah. Yeah, I guess so."

"Where'd you know him from?"

Artemis tensed now. There was something unnerving about the casual way Forester was asking the question.

"He's just an old family friend," she said, her voice guarded. "We've known him for a long time."

Forester raised an eyebrow. "Just an old family friend? He seems to have a pretty unique skill set."

"He's a hypnotherapist," Artemis said, her tone clipped. "He's helped us out before."

Forester nodded, but she could tell he wasn't convinced. "Alright," he said, his tone noncommittal. "Well, I guess we'll see what he can do with this guy."

Artemis nodded, her gaze still fixed on the interrogation room. She could see her father's hands moving in slow, soothing motions, and Javail's sobs had grown quieter.

"He's good," she said, almost to herself. "He's really good."

Forester looked at her again, his expression unreadable. "You trust him?"

She hesitated then nodded. "Yeah. Yeah, I do."

But even as she said the words, a small voice in the back of her mind whispered doubts. Her father was a master manipulator—What if he was manipulating her, too?

Artemis pushed the thoughts aside.

She tried not to look at Cameron but could feel him watching her still.

He said, "Was he a friend of your father's?"

The words came quick as if he'd been holding them back.

She looked sharply at him, and he held up both hands. "It's no big deal. Really. I get if you're embarrassed about it. I'd be too. Just curious is all."

She bit her lip, staring. Forester thought this man was connected to the Ghost Killer. He didn't have a clue who it really was.

Partly, she felt relieved.

But another part of her felt a surge of guilt as she lied with a noncommittal shrug. "Yeah. Just not worth mentioning."

"Heard anything about Otto since he escaped?" Forester said, casually glancing through the glass once more.

"Nothing," she said. "I'd turn him in if I had."

"Yeah. Yeah, I know." Forester scowled, shaking his head and rubbing his knuckles. "Guys that hurt young women really piss me off, Artemis. I know he's your old man... but if I got my hands on him, let's just say there might not be much left *to* arrest."

She frowned even more deeply but held her tongue and cleared her throat. "We should look into wolf permits."

"How's that?"

She said, a bit more firmly, "We should look into anyone who has access to wolves. Especially in mental health fields in the surrounding area. We can cross-reference that with the financial statements of the victims. We need to check Javail's cards too. Another data point."

Forester was nodding. "You're sure this guy has a wolf?"

"No, but it's a lead. My dad's, er, *friend* seems to think so."

"You really trust him that much?"

"Yeah. Where's your computer? They're going to be a few minutes in there."

"Fine. Sure." Forester shrugged, staring at her. For a moment, he shifted awkwardly from one foot to the other.

"What?" she said.

"Nothing just..." He scratched at the back of his head, turned away from the window now. "I just wasn't sure what I did."

"Excuse me?"

He shifted again from one foot to the other. "What I did," he repeated. "A few weeks ago you were into me, yeah? Well... I mean, technically, I was—"

"Yikes, okay, I get it. I don't want to talk about it now, Cameron."

He nodded quickly. "Sure, sure, yeah..." He began glancing back to the window in the direction of her father.

She felt a flare of panic, and if only to redirect his gaze, she blurted out, "I think you're hot."

His gaze snapped back to her.

The two of them stood alone in the corridor. She took a step forward, pushing him away from the door. Partly, so he couldn't keep watching her father, but also so her father wouldn't watch them.

She was nodding, though, trying to keep his attention, while also feeling a warm flush along her face. "You're hot, but you scare me, Cameron."

"You said that before, and I told you I'd keep my distance."

"You didn't really, though, did you?"

"I'm not the one who snuck into your shower."

"I didn't sneak!" she retorted. "I just..." She bit her lip, staring off down the hall. "We should focus on the case. We can talk about this later."

Forester shrugged. "Okay."

"Good."

"No more talking."

"Right."

She began to turn, but he snagged her wrist. In one quick motion, he pulled her close and leaned in, his tall frame stretching above her. He wasn't rough where he held her wrist but, rather, his fingers stroked gently at her hand.

He hesitated for only the briefest second, leaning in, his eyes half-hooded as he stared at her. He seemed to be waiting to see if she'd pull away.

She didn't.

So he kissed her.

It was soft and gentle, but she could feel the longing and need in it. His lips moved hungrily against hers.

When he pulled away, her entire body felt electric. She was aware of his hand still holding her wrist gently, and his breath against her face.

He smiled and brushed a thumb across her cheek.

"God dammit," she whispered.

"How sweet," he returned, his breath warm against her face.

She shook her head, closing her eyes, her lips tingling. She wanted to kiss him back. It was a strange realization.

Artemis hadn't dated for years. She'd avoided all romantic entanglements. It had felt too dangerous—as if she were setting herself up to lose another loved one.

But then Jamie had come along...

And she'd chosen her sister over him, so he'd left.

And now, standing there, a man she was lying to.

She wasn't telling him the truth about her sister, about her father... about any of it.

But another part of her didn't think he'd care.

"You know," Forester said quietly, "I've been thinking—"

She didn't want to hear it. So she leaned in, just as quick, kissing him back.

This time, they didn't withdraw for what felt like minutes.

The soft press of his lips against hers, the warmth of his body, the way he held her close.

She felt something spark between them and her heart raced.

When they finally pulled away, both of them were breathing heavily.

Forester looked down at her, his eyes searching her face for something. "Artemis... I don't want to hurt you."

She lightly touched his face. "I don't want to talk about it."

He nodded, a slight smile playing on his lips. "We should get back to work then."

"Yeah," she said, stepping back to give him some space.

He cleared his throat, glancing away. "Right. I'll just... get the computer."

He stepped towards the breakroom, shooting her a hesitant glance as if scared she might evaporate. But Artemis sighed, trying to quell her spinning thoughts.

That was the scariest part...

Thinking hadn't been involved at all. Just instinct. Pure, physical instinct.

Cameron made her feel safe in some ways... and terrified in others.

She fell into step, following after him, her heart still pounding.

She still wasn't sure what to do about her feelings.

But perhaps the lack of certainty wasn't a bad thing anyway.

Perhaps it just *was.*

She shook her head, a finger grazing her lip, and she lowered her head, moving hastily after the tall agent.

They still had a killer to catch.

And he only seemed to be escalating.

The question that now buzzed in her mind was a simple one: who was going to die next?

CHAPTER 22

Neither of them discussed the kiss as they stared at the computer, and Artemis could feel her excitement mounting as the list narrowed further.

"No one who's outside a counseling profession," she said quickly. "For this to work, he would've needed access."

Forester paused, clicked a button on the screen and the colors changed.

He leaned back, the chair creaking as his left hand's fingers drummed against the break room table. "Now what?" he muttered.

She bit her lip, hesitant, frowning at the results. "How many?"

"A couple thousand in the state."

"Really? That many people own wolves?"

"Nah. Can't own 'em, but have access to them. Animal shelters, rehabilitation areas, vets—you name it. Two thousand with access and some involvement in counseling or therapy."

Artemis frowned, leaning against the break room table, staring at the screen. Then, she said, "Caucasian?"

"We know that for sure?"

"My dad's friend seemed pretty confident."

Forester shrugged, clicked another button. The list narrowed further. "A thousand five hundred results left," he said.

"Alright... Umm... Any way to narrow based on hair length?"

"Not really. I mean, we can go in manually and look."

"Alright... that's a long list. Did you narrow the radius within fifty miles?"

He glanced at her. "You sure we don't want to check the state?" For a moment, his eyes lingered on her, and she felt her lips tingle. A warmth spread through her chest, but she quickly pushed the emotion aside. She shook her head. "No. It would be someone in close proximity. They showed up at the door to two of the locations. I'm sure of it. Make them local."

"That'll take a big chunk out of the could-bes." He clicked another button, dragged a slider, and then whistled. "Only fifty-five in the Cascades, near the winery."

"Good." She was nodding now, feeling her excitement rising. "Let's see if any of them have long hair."

Forester pulled up DMV photos, and one by one, they browsed through.

Artemis hesitated at one image, then said, "Better safe than sorry, but wait, no... Javail said the ghost was pale."

"The ghost was..." Forester snorted. "This is all getting to be too much."

"Just trust me."

He shrugged, dragging the name off the compiled list and clicking through the second page of results in the database.

Artemis shifted from foot to foot, her excitement rising.

And then someone knocked on the door.

She whirled around, heart leaping, expecting to find her father peering through the smudged glass of the breakroom window.

But it wasn't Otto.

Instead, Dr. Bryant was staring at them, gesturing earnestly at Artemis.

"What do you think she wants?" Forester murmured, still clicking through the narrowed list.

"I... let me check. Can you do this on your own? Err on the side of safety. If you think they're a match at all, keep them."

"Yeah, yeah," Forester said, continuing to sort through the list. He turned briefly to watch her leave, though, and she could feel his eyes on her body as she hastened away.

She felt a strange shiver down her back at his gaze. Forester never pretended to be anything he wasn't.

She wondered if she could do the same.

Thoughts of the ogling FBI agent were quickly replaced as Artemis pushed through the door and stepped into the hall to face Dr. Bryant.

Miracle's hair was now, strangely, its normal, dark brown hue. The locks were curly instead of straightened. She hadn't applied makeup this morning, and even her shirt was a dull gray.

For a brief second, Artemis was taken aback by the woman's appearance. She still had her paste-on nails and eyelashes, but her eyes—normally so full of life—were dull.

She looked weary as if she'd been crying.

Artemis' heart panged. "Is everything okay?" she whispered.

Miracle bit her lip but nodded. "I'm sorry for bothering you like this, my dear, but... I just didn't know who else to turn to."

"Of course," Artemis said quickly. "Of course," she repeated more firmly, emphasizing both words. "How can I help?"

Miracle was shaking her head, running a hand over her face. "I keep going over it, and... and I just don't know how to help my brother. Is he..." She shifted nervously. "Is he ever going to be the same again?"

Artemis blinked. She stared at the woman, then realized Miracle was holding back tears.

"Oh..." Artemis said simply. She hesitated. Then, despite her instincts, she leaned in and gave the woman a quick side hug.

Miracle broke down, crying now, resting her head against Artemis' shoulder. "I'm sorry," Dr. Bryant kept repeating. "I'm sorry. I promise I'm normally much better at keeping my emotions in check. Just ask Desmond."

Artemis hesitated at the mention of Forester's partner. Desmond Wade had been on a call with Miracle a few weeks ago and had quickly disconnected. She'd wondered if the two had been secretly flirting.

Then again, office romance was no one's business, was it?

She refused to glance over her shoulder or to acknowledge the bias in the thought.

Instead, she just held the kind-hearted, middle-aged woman. A woman who'd gone out of her way to help others on more than one occasion.

"It's going to be okay," Artemis said in a soothing voice.

"It's... it's just I never thought we'd go through something like this again with Benjamin. He'd been sober for nearly a decade. He... he had some trouble growing up, but he really turned things around, and I... I can't help but think I'm going to lose him."

Artemis shook her head. "If I can prove he was hypnotized, coerced into this, then I'm sure we can get him off."

"But his wife..."

Artemis shook her head. "I know. I know, but he can heal. Right now, all I can do is find out who was behind this."

She was leaning back now, holding Miracle at arm's length. "It's the best shot we have," Artemis said, firmly.

Miracle nodded, wiping her tears with a tissue. "Thank you, Artemis. I know I can always count on you."

Artemis smiled, her heart swelling with pride. She was glad to be able to help someone in need, especially someone like Miracle.

Just then, her phone buzzed in her pocket. She pulled it out and saw a text from Forester. "Found a match. Meet me outside."

She shot a quick look into the break room and realized Forester had left, taking the door in the opposite wall.

She frowned.

After a quick hug, and a few more encouraging words, Artemis quickly excused herself from Miracle and rushed out of the building. She found Forester leaning against his car, a file in his hand.

"Okay, spill," Artemis said, eagerly.

Forester grinned, holding up the file. "Meet our guy. Lucas Reynolds. Lives just a few miles away from the winery. Long hair. Caucasian. And get this, he's a therapist who specializes in animal-assisted therapy."

Artemis felt a thrill run through her body. "This could be it," she said, taking the file from him.

Forester nodded, his eyes sparkling with excitement. "Let's pay him a visit."

Artemis paused, staring at the name. "Were there others on the list?"

"None that met the criteria and were still in state. A couple are retired. A couple more are on vacation. A few are women."

"Right," Artemis said. "So... Lucas Reynolds."

She frowned, staring at the image on Forester's phone. The man in question had a creepy smile and his eyes seemed to bore into her soul. It made her skin crawl. His face was as pale as snow, and his sheer black hair—as dark as her own—hung down to his shoulders. He wore glasses and an arrogant smile.

She felt a shiver down her spine as she met the intelligent eyes staring back at her.

"I'll drive!" Forester called out, already slipping into the front seat of the car.

CHAPTER 23

The animal therapist's home was a small, cozy house on the outskirts of town. A couple of acres of land surrounded the house, and Artemis could see a couple of horses grazing in the distance.

"Horses," she said as they moved up the gravel driveway. "Any sign of a wolf?"

Forester just shook his head, frowning towards the house. "I don't like that..." he muttered.

"What is it?"

She followed his gaze and spotted a figure sitting framed in the window of the top floor, staring down at them.

At first, she'd taken the figure for a gargoyle or some stone construct it was sitting so still. But as they drew up the driveway, she realized the dark silhouette was the outline of a *very* large man.

Now that she noticed it, she realized the horses were also quite large.

The steps up to the house were sturdy, and the door frame itself looked custom-made, as if it were intentionally stretched to give room for someone of a larger frame.

She felt her skin prickle as she stared at the giant on the second floor leering down at them.

He didn't blink. Didn't move.

A dog lay at his side, and the enormous man's thick fingers combed through the dog's shaggy fur.

Artemis and Forester tentatively emerged from their vehicle, peering up at the figure.

Artemis raised a hand in greeting, if only to help defuse some of the tension she was feeling.

The greeting was not returned.

"Think we should call for backup?" Artemis whispered under her breath.

Forester hesitated, then frowned at her. He puffed his chest a bit as he adjusted his belt. He shut the car door with his heel and then began moving up the gravel with crunching steps. "You think I can't take him?"

"It's not that," she said quietly. "Besides, hopefully we don't have to *take* him."

"Think a hypnotist murderer is gonna come quietly?" Forester replied.

Artemis sighed, joining him on the steps. "Please, Cameron, you don't have to do anything to impress me."

He looked at her and frowned. Then pointed at her face, opened his mouth, and couldn't think of anything to say. So he turned, pounding his fist against the door.

"Lucas Reynolds!" Forester called out. "Open up, FBI! Open up, now!"

Silence greeted them. Artemis peered up at the top of the elongated doorframe, struck again at how the door didn't quite fit the dimensions of the wall.

Her eyes moved to boots by the door. Caked in mud and filth, smelling of horse manure, the boots were as long as her shin.

She stared, feeling a slow prickle of worry creeping along her back. The shoes had to be at least four times the size of her own.

She glanced at her feet, up again.

"Are you *sure* we don't need backup?" she whispered.

But Cameron seemed to take the concern personally. He pounded the door a bit more, still yelling. "Come on, now!" he shouted. "Open up! FBI!"

There was a pause, and then the sound of heavy footfalls coming from above them. Thick steps. Then voices. Plural.

Artemis hesitated. "Does... does Lucas live with anyone?"

Forester paused, glanced at his phone, checked a link then looked up again. "His brother. I guess his brother is kinda his caretaker. At least, claimed him as a dependent on his last tax return."

Artemis felt a chill now.

The voices were drawing closer, along with the sound of thumping footsteps.

In her mind, the words resonated: fee-fi-fo-fum.

She shivered, glancing along the side of the house and half expecting to find a beanstalk.

Suddenly, the door creaked open, and a gruff voice emanated from inside. "What do you want?"

Forester took a step forward, flashing his badge, peering through the open crack in the door. Within, the hall was dark. And the outline of the figure was hard to discern. "We're here to speak with Lucas Reynolds," Forester said.

The figure in the doorway loomed over them, his massive frame casting a long shadow. "Why?" he growled.

"We have reason to believe he may have information on a case we're working on," Artemis interjected, trying to keep her voice steady.

The man's eyes narrowed, and he scrutinized them for a long moment before shaking his head. "No," he said simply. And then he shut the door in Cameron's face.

Forester blinked then scowled. He raised his face, pounding on the door again, even louder.

This time, the door flung open, and they were treated to their first look at a seven-foot-tall, musclebound giant of a man.

His dark hair was cropped short, his beard thick and black. His face was stern, and his eyes were a piercing blue. He wore a plain white t-shirt that stretched tightly over his brawny chest and bulging biceps. His jeans looked like they had been ripped and repaired multiple times but still managed to cling to his tree-trunk legs.

"What part of 'no' don't you understand?" he boomed, his voice echoing through the hallway. Then, as if uncertain they got the message, he added a glare.

Artemis couldn't help but take a step back as the man towered over them.

"We just have—" she began, but his face was twisted into a scowl, and his eyes seemed to bore into her.

"I said no," he repeated, his voice like thunder.

"We're with the FBI," Forester said, standing his ground. "We have a warrant to search this property."

The giant scoffed, crossing his massive arms over his chest. "I don't believe you," he said, his eyes flickering over to Artemis. "Who's the little lady?"

"I'm Artemis," she said, trying to keep her voice steady. "We're just trying to do our job here."

The giant raised an eyebrow. "And what job is that?"

"We're investigating a series of murders," Forester said. "We believe Lucas Reynolds may have information that could help us catch the killer. Is that you? Or is it your brother?"

The giant snorted. "Lucas ain't got nothing to do with that," he said. "Now get off my property before I make you."

Artemis blinked in surprise at the open threat. Forester bristled. "So you're not Lucas? That must make you Georgie."

"Yeah? So what?" the man demanded, pushing out his chin. "My lil bro hasn't hurt nobody."

Forester scowled. "He's an animal therapist?"

Here, the giant just frowned. He hesitated, scratched at his cheek, then glanced back over his muscled shoulder as if searching for someone. In a quieter voice, as if fearful he might be overheard, he said, "My lil bro passed the test, but he doesn't practice. Can't. Don't got the upstairs for it." He tapped a thick digit against his temple. Then, as if feeling he'd revealed too much, he scowled again, adding another growl, "Get off my property. NOW!"

"Lucas?" Forester called past the man. "Lucas Reynolds, is this really how you want to play it? Hmm? Get big bro to fight your battles for you? Wuss."

Artemis winced.

The giant in the doorway bristled. He raised a fist, but just then, a new voice joined the throng.

This one more timid, hesitant.

A faint voice that probed out from the dark. "Who is it, Georgie?" said the voice.

Artemis had heard voices like that before. The use of steroids could affect the cadence of a voice. And now, she stared as a new figure emerged.

This one stepped from the shadows as if emerging from a pool of ink.

And stunningly, he was even larger than his enormous brother. And he was built like a brick wall, with more muscles under his bright yellow muscle shirt than she'd ever seen.

He looked like he could bench press a car. His bald head gleamed in the dim light, and his piercing green eyes fixed on the FBI agents with a mixture of curiosity and suspicion.

"Who are you people?" he demanded, his high-pitched voice tremoring.

"We're with the FBI," Forester said again, holding up his badge. "We need to speak with Lucas Reynolds. Now. I'm guessing that's you, big guy."

This second giant's eyes narrowed, and he crossed his bulky arms over his chest. He had no hair, no eyebrows. And there was a timid look in his eyes that didn't match his physique.

The first giant, Georgie, jutted his black beard at them, though, snapping, "I told you he's got nothing to do with this."

"We believe he may have information," Artemis said, trying to keep her voice steady and diplomatic. She couldn't help but feel intimidated standing in front of these two behemoths.

The bald giant looked them up and down, his gaze lingering on Artemis for a moment longer than necessary. She felt a shiver run down her spine.

"Well, you're not gonna find him here," Georgie said finally, turning to go back into the darkness.

"Not gonna find him, huh? And who's this guy? Your wife?"

"Shut up, pipsqueak."

Georgie began to shut the door, but Forester blocked it with his foot.

"Lucas," Forester said, staring at the bald giant. "Why don't we have a chat, huh?"

But Georgie snapped, "Leave before I get angry."

Forester stepped forward, his eyes hard. "Listen, we have a warrant to search this property," he said. "Stop playing. Lucas," Forester added, peering past the big brother. "We just have to talk. Just a few questions."

Artemis' mind was spinning. She wasn't sure how any of this would go down.

Forester was an ex-cage-fighter. He knew how to handle himself in a scuffle. But against two leviathans like this?

She felt a shiver creep along her back.

Georgie tried to slam the door.

Forester refused to move his foot. Georgie tried to shove the agent, and Forester moved fast. Far faster than Artemis could track.

One moment, the giant was shoving the agent, the next, his arm was yanked forward, and he was sent sprawling down the stairs.

CHAPTER 24

Georgie, the 'little' brother, cracked one of the porch steps with his great girth as he careened into it, letting out a grunt of pain as he hit the asphalt at the base of the stairs. And then, all hell broke loose.

The bald giant stepped forward, his muscles rippling under his shirt as he bared his teeth in a snarl. He charged at Forester, his massive fists swinging in a wild arc.

Artemis could barely keep up with the movements as the two men collided, exchanging blows that sounded like gunshots in the enclosed space.

Georgie, meanwhile, had staggered to his feet, his eyes blazing with fury as he charged at Artemis. She stumbled backward, tripping over her own feet and landing hard on the concrete.

She scrambled back, her heart pounding in her chest as Georgie loomed over her like a mountain.

But just as she thought he was going to strike her, there was a sudden blur of movement.

Forester had grabbed Georgie by the back of his shirt, pulling him away from Artemis with a strength that made her gasp.

But this put him between the two brothers. And now, he had to face both of them as they tried to bring him to the ground.

Forester was taken to the ground under a mountain of muscle and bulk. He shouted as he hit the floor, splintering the deck. Forester didn't pause, though.

Sometimes, Artemis forgot who he really was.

What he was capable of.

Now, as he was slammed to the ground, he twisted wildly, wrapping his legs around one of the giant's necks. He used the same motion to snatch at the other's wrist, bending the fingers back.

Georgie howled as his hand twisted, and Lucas grunted, trying to disentangle from where Forester's legs wrapped around his neck.

Forester used the new position to leverage himself back up into a standing position.

He didn't slow, either.

Artemis tried to push at Georgie, but he back-handed her, sending her tumbling back into the railing.

Forester howled, redoubling his efforts.

The ex-fighter and self-proclaimed sociopath's fists were a blur as he landed powerful punches on the bald giant's face and chest. Lucas stumbled back, but recovered quickly, landing a heavy blow on Forester's side.

Artemis watched in horror as Forester grunted in pain, but he didn't back down. He continued to fight with everything he had, landing blow after blow on the giant. But the two brothers were too strong, too resilient. They kept coming, fists pounding into Forester's flesh like sledgehammers.

Artemis knew she had to do something. She couldn't just stand there and watch Forester get beaten to a pulp. Taking a deep breath, she stepped forward, her heart racing with fear and adrenaline.

Artemis steeled herself. She stepped forward and landed a powerful kick on the bald giant's knee, using the technique Forester had taught her while training.

Her shin connected and lanced with pain.

But Lucas grunted and stumbled back, giving Forester an opening to deliver a devastating punch to his jaw.

The giant fell to the ground with a thump.

Breathless, Artemis looked at Forester, her heart pounding in her chest.

Now, only Georgie remained.

"Come on then!" Forester howled, spittle flecking the giant's face as the two of them grappled.

They smashed into the railing, sending bits of wood and splinters flying.

They fell straight through and into the garden.

They rolled on the ground, and Artemis shouted. "Stop! Stop now!"

But Georgie didn't listen.

He was now trying to strangle Forester. Artemis knew she had to act fast. She scanned the area for anything she could use as a weapon. Her eyes landed on a nearby garden tool shed. Without hesitation, she sprinted towards it, her heart pounding in her chest. She flung open the door and quickly grabbed a shovel.

As she turned to run back to the fight, she felt a strong hand grab her arm. She screamed and turned to face Lucas, who had managed to get back on his feet.

"You're not going anywhere," he growled, tightening his grip on her arm as the two of them watched his brother fight Forester.

Lucas was bleeding from his nose, and one of his eyes had blackened.

Artemis tried to wriggle free, but his grip was too strong. She felt a surge of panic rise in her throat.

But then she remembered something Forester had taught her.

She stepped forward, putting her body weight into her left foot. She twisted her right leg around and kicked up, her heel connecting with Lucas' shin. The giant grunted and released his grip on her arm.

Seizing the opportunity, Artemis swung the shovel at Lucas' head. It connected with a sickening thud, and he crumpled to the ground.

Breathless, Artemis turned to Forester who was still grappling Georgie. The sheer size of the brute was giving Cameron some difficulty. His face was red, and he emitted a gagging sound due to the fingers wrapped around his neck.

Artemis grabbed a nearby garden hose and ran towards the two men. "Let him go!" she shouted, spraying Georgie in the face with the hose. The sudden rush of water blinded him for a moment, and he loosened his grip on Forester.

Forester took the opportunity to land a powerful punch to Georgie's face. The giant grunted, trying to blink the water free.

She sprayed him again.

Forester managed to rise, slipping in mud, but with a snarl, he brought his knee up and in, slamming it into the giant's chin.

Finally, Georgie let out a grunt then toppled like a felled Redwood, hitting the ground and splashing in the mud.

Artemis stared, heart hammering in her chest, as Forester stood up, panting and covered in blood and dirt.

"Are you okay?" she asked, running towards him.

Forester nodded, his chest heaving as he caught his breath. "Yeah, I'm fine," he said, wiping the blood from his mouth. "Thanks for the assist."

Artemis nodded, a sense of relief flooding through her. "Can we call for backup now?" she said, pulling out her phone.

Forester nodded, glancing down at the unconscious giants. "Meh," he said. "We had it handled. Like I said. Here, I need the extra cuffs from the back seat. His wrists are too thick." She hastened to the car, retrieving the handcuffs and returning them to him.

The metal bracelets clicked into place on Georgie's wrists first, and then another doubled pair on Lucas'.

Forester glanced at the shovel next to Lucas' unconscious form.

"Damn. Nice hit."

She blushed. "Thanks. Umm..." She glanced at her phone again. "Paramedics are on the way."

Forester shook his head, staring at her. "Just like you..."

"What?"

His tone wasn't hostile, though, but more like admiration. "To think of paramedics first. You're actually worried about these guys?"

She shrugged. "They're hurt."

Forester shook his head side to side. "Damn... Their heads are too thick. They'll be fine. Hey, before they get here," he said quickly as if adding an afterthought, "Why don't we check things out. You know, look around real quick. They're not going anywhere in their state."

Artemis frowned. Forester gestured towards the house. "I have a feeling we might find something worth fighting over in the house."

"Maybe... watch out for a wolf, though."

"Yeah, shit. Right. I forgot about the wolf. You coming?"

She glanced back at the two cuffed, unconscious men. Forester had cuffed their ankles together as well. They wouldn't be running any time soon.

She sighed, and Forester said.

"Here, if it'll make you feel better, we can lock 'em in the back seat first. Better hurry before backup arrives, though."

Reluctantly she nodded and helped Forester heft the two giants into the back seat of the car.

She grimaced at the weight, her arms and back straining.

It took some doing, but eventually, both men were stuffed in the back seats.

As they locked the car doors, Artemis couldn't shake off the uneasy feeling in her gut. She knew that Forester was right. There was something in that house that was worth fighting over, but she couldn't help but feel like they were walking into a trap.

CHAPTER 25

They approached the house cautiously, looking for any signs of danger. As they circled around the side of the house, Artemis felt a sudden gust of wind. She shivered, feeling a chill run down her spine.

Forester must have felt it too because he stopped in his tracks, turning to face her. "You alright?" he asked, his voice low and concerned.

Artemis nodded, but she couldn't shake off the feeling of unease. "Yeah, I'm fine," she said, her voice barely above a whisper.

Forester gave her a reassuring nod and motioned for her to follow him. They approached the back door of the house, and Forester pulled out a set of lockpicks.

She stared. "Do you usually carry lockpicks?"

He winked. "Lighter and knife too. Never know when you need one. Here, give me a sec. How long until backup, by the way?"

"Shit," she muttered under her breath.

She ducked back out into the hall, and that's when she heard the growling.

Disturbed, it seemed, by the sound of the cat, the growling was now coming from the locked door she'd tried.

Forester was emerging from a room at the far end, wrinkling his nose in disgust, and kicking at a piece of toilet paper that had stuck to his foot. Once he'd freed himself from the damp paper, he looked at her, shaking his head.

"Nothing. You find anything?"

"Just a cat," she whispered. "But listen."

She pointed to the room with a low, grumbling sound. Lucas was registered as an animal therapist, but according to his brother, he didn't practice. Having interacted with both brothers, Artemis doubted very much that either of them had the capacity for counseling of any variety.

But they did have a permit for dangerous creatures.

The growling continued.

"Think it's a wolf?" she whispered.

Forester approached slowly, finger to his lips, his eyes on the closed, locked door.

"We should be careful," she said quickly.

In the distance, she thought she heard sirens. Which meant backup was nearly there.

"Maybe we should wait," she began.

But Forester's lockpicks had emerged once more, and he was already probing at the keyhole with quiet scraping sounds of the metal instruments.

Artemis held her breath as Forester worked on the lock, her eyes darting nervously around the hallway. The growling was getting louder and more vicious, and she could feel her pulse racing in her veins.

She wanted to tell Forester to stop, to wait for backup, but she knew that they didn't have much time.

Finally, with a soft click, Forester managed to unlock the door. He motioned for her to stand back as he slowly pushed it open.

They both peered inside, Forester's gun at the ready.

The room was dimly lit, but Artemis could make out a large shape in the corner. As her eyes adjusted to the darkness, she discerned the thing's form.

The animal was massive, with thick, shaggy fur and glowing, amber eyes. It was baring its teeth, snarling and growling in a low, menacing tone.

Artemis felt a sudden surge of fear, and she took a step back.

"Shit," she whispered. "What do we do now?"

Forester didn't answer. He was staring intently at the wolf, his gun held steady in his hand.

Suddenly, the animal lunged forward, its jaws snapping shut with a loud, teeth-clattering sound.

Artemis stumbled backwards, her heart racing in her chest.

But Forester didn't move. He was still staring at the wolf, his expression unconcerned.

The creature bounded across the room, but only made it a few steps before it was yanked back.

She spotted the gleam of a chain as it rattled from the fixture anchoring it to the wall.

The wolf snarled and snapped, sending spittle flecking across the ground, but it couldn't reach them, held back as it was by the chain.

Forester took a step forward, his gun trained away from the massive creature as if he couldn't quite bring himself to point the weapon at the chained animal. "We need to get it out of here," he said, his voice low and steady. "Somewhere safe."

Artemis blinked in surprise. Sweat prickled across her brow. This hadn't been the first thought to cross her mind. Forester was staring at the wolf with something like sympathy in his gaze.

He massaged at his own neck, eyeing the chain wrapped around the beast's neck.

"Isn't right keeping a wild thing locked up like that."

It was perhaps predictable coming from the man who still couldn't quite figure out how to properly button his suit.

But Artemis nodded, her heart still pounding in her chest. They had to be careful. One wrong move and that wolf would tear them apart.

Forester slowly approached the wolf, his gun held steady, and Artemis followed close behind. The animal growled and snapped, but it couldn't break free from the chain.

As they got closer, Artemis could see that the wolf's fur was matted and dirty, its eyes wild with fear and anger. It was obvious that it hadn't been taken care of properly.

"We need to calm it down," she said quietly. "Or... or we could wait for animal control."

"Nah. They'll just put it down. Wild thing like this? No. Only way it lives is if we release it in the mountains."

She stared at the side of his face. "Release it?"

"Lotta wolves around these parts," he said, frowning, his expression stubborn.

Artemis just stared at the creature, her skin prickling. She wasn't sure if she should interject.

She could see this mattered to Forester.

She remembered the kiss...

Had things really changed between them?

She frowned.

In the distance, she heard sirens approaching, still a ways off, but coming ever closer.

He looked at her now, and Forester held her gaze. There was a pleading note to his voice. "Please... Help me get this thing out of it."

There was something in his eyes she couldn't quite place, but her heart melted, and she nodded. "Alright," she murmured. "But we need to calm it first."

The wolf was still snarling, growling, but it had retreated now, fearful of the two figures facing it, and perturbed that they weren't frightened of it.

Forester nodded in agreement. "I'll try to distract it," he said. "You see if you can find something to calm it down."

Artemis nodded and quickly scanned the room. For the two giants to control the wild thing, they would've needed some help.

Part of their permit also allowed them to have controlled substances for helping to keep their animal sedated.

She frowned, and said, "One sec."

Hastily, she returned to the bathroom, held her nose, and ventured in.

She tried not to look around too much, but the place was a dumpster fire and smelled like a sewer.

It had a medicine cabinet, though.

She opened it, her eyes jumping across the bottles. Then...

She spotted it.

"Yes!" she exclaimed, pumping her first. There was a small bottle of sedative on the lowest shelf, and she grabbed it. She returned to the room with Forester, twisted off the cap, and slowly approached the wolf, holding the bottle out in front of her.

The wolf snarled and lunged forward, but Forester stepped in front, his gun still trained off to the side of the animal.

Artemis quickly sprayed the sedative into the air, hoping that it would calm the wolf down.

At first, there was no response. The wolf continued to growl and snap, its eyes fixed on Forester. But then, slowly, it began to calm down. Its growls became softer, and its eyes lost their wildness.

The droplets of moisture landed on its muzzle, and it sneezed.

Then, it began moving slower, still growling, but its eyes drooping.

"Looks like it's working," Cameron whispered excitement in his voice.

Artemis nodded, her heart racing with equal parts fear and adrenaline. She took a tentative step closer to the wolf, her hand outstretched. The creature didn't snap or growl but merely watched her with glazed eyes.

"We need to get it out of here," Forester said, his voice low and urgent. "Before the cops arrive."

Artemis nodded, reaching down to unhook the chain from the wall. The wolf didn't seem to resist as she led it out of the room, Forester following close behind.

They made their way down the hallway and out the back door of the dingy house, the wolf stumbling along behind them. Artemis could feel its weight against her as she struggled to keep it upright.

"Where are we going?" she asked, her voice shaking slightly.

Forester didn't answer, but instead led them deeper into the woods. The wolf was fully sedated now, its eyes closed as it breathed softly against her side, moving with only the slowest of motions.

Finally, they came to a clearing at the base of the mountain only a couple minutes from the house. Forester set down his gun and reached for the chain, slowly unhooking it from the wolf's neck.

The creature stirred slightly but didn't move as Forester stepped away.

"Come on," he said, motioning for Artemis to follow. "Let's go."

She hesitated, staring at the wolf as it lay there, its breathing shallow and slow.

"What if it wakes up?" she asked, her voice barely above a whisper. "What if it attacks someone else?"

Forester shrugged. "It won't hurt anybody," he said. "At least... no more than any of the other wolves in these mountains. There's thousands of them. Not fair to turn this guy over to an injection just cuz a couple of assholes had him chained up."

Artemis bit on the corner of her lip. She stared at where the wolf was now laying docile. It let out a faint whimpering sound as it spotted the chain loose in Forester's hand.

She wasn't sure if the wolf understood what was happening.

But Cameron didn't seem to care.

He had already turned and was hastening back in the direction of their parked vehicle and the two suspects they'd left in the back seat.

Artemis paused, frowning now, picturing the medicine cabinet in her mind. There had been other items in there as well.

Not just the sedative... but bottles with labels.

"What's scopolamine?" she said.

He paused, turning back to look at her. Sirens were now at the house, and through the trees, she spotted flashing lights.

But Forester didn't seem to be in a hurry. He still gripped the chain but now watched her with a curious look. "Where did you hear that word?"

"Is it bad?"

"It's an illegal drug. A criminal's drug, they say. Supposedly," Forester said, rubbing at his jaw and shaking his head, "It's supposed to take over the free will of another person. A powerful sedative that allows predators and criminals to control others."

"Is it used on animals or people?"

"Both, probably."

Artemis shivered. She cursed.

"What?"

"Then I know why they picked a fight with us."

"Those two bozos?"

She nodded, rubbing her hands together and feeling a chill. "Yeah. They had bottles of the stuff upstairs."

"Bottles of it?"

"At least ten."

"Shit... Dealers, then."

She sighed, rubbing at the bridge of her nose. "Double shit, Cameron."

"Why?"

"Because it explains why the two of them would lash out. But also... if they had the means to control someone, why use hypnosis at all?"

Forester frowned. "What are you saying?"

"I don't think the giants are the killers. I think they're criminals, but they're too stupid to hypnotize anyone." She was nodding adamantly. "They were protecting their stash, and they could've just used the drugs instead of going to the lengths of hypnotizing someone." Then, she slapped a fist into her palm. "Dammit."

"What now."

"I've been stupid."

"Never seen it. Don't believe it."

"No, really. It's... It's what my father used to say." She swallowed and felt a flicker of fear. She'd been about to say it was what her father said. But Forester didn't notice the slip so she continued. "Someone has to be willing and open and vulnerable to be hypnotized. Do you think either Georgie or Lucas would've put *any* of the victims at ease?"

Forester scratched at his chin, the chain in one hand swaying slightly. He winced but then gave a faint shake of his head.

"Shit," he said. "But... they still might be our guys."

"You can speak to them," she said quickly. "But I have a bad feeling, Cameron... I don't think they're involved in this. I think we missed it."

"So why do you have that look in your eyes?"

259

"What look?"

"That one."

"I don't have a look."

A voice now calling out behind them. An officer waving in their direction. The man was from the precinct they'd been using and recognized them, frowning and calling them over.

Artemis lowered her voice as the two of them began to move in the direction of the cop.

"Those drugs..." she said quietly. "It's given me an idea. I don't know how I didn't see it before."

"What idea?"

"You should interrogate the two giants. Just to be sure."

"What are you going to do?"

"I need to talk to Benjamin Clarkson."

"Why?"

"Just... it's probably nothing. But I think I might know how they were all hypnotized."

Chapter 26

Artemis had returned to the interrogation room, and this time, she didn't look in Benjamin's direction.

She was staring at the backs of her hands, thinking through how she wanted to approach the subject.

Already, things were going poorly in the next-door interrogation room, where the two giants had provided solid alibis for the second murder—both of them had been at a cattle auction. Due to their size, many of the auctioneers and attendees had remembered the men.

But Artemis was more convinced than ever, now, that she was onto something.

She remembered the twitchy way in which the two hypnotized victims had sat.

She'd thought it had been due to the hypnosis, but now she was wondering if she'd missed something.

She thought of the drugs in the cabinet. Thought of the mention of a *group*.

She didn't look up, didn't want him to feel confronted, but then softly said, "Do you have a drug issue?"

Benjamin balked. He didn't reply at first. She was still staring at her hands.

He shifted uncomfortably, his chair scraping against the ground, the handcuffs rattling around his wrists.

"Wh-what?" he stammered.

She looked up now, trying to communicate an air of gentleness. "I'm not trying to embarrass you. I just need to know. Do you have a drug issue? More importantly, did you attend groups for it? Anything? AA? Something similar?"

He stared at her as if he'd been slapped, then his eyes slipped to the door, as if searching for someone.

"Your sister isn't here," Artemis said, guessing at the reason for his hesitation. "She's getting some much-needed sleep. She cares about you a lot, Benjamin. She's been crying. She mentioned to me, back in the day, you'd had issues with drugs. I didn't make the connection at first. That's my fault."

He continued to stare at her, wetting his lips as he did. He stammered but then shook his head.

"Is that a yes?"

In a ghost of a voice, he murmured, "I don't use anymore, but I still attend the groups."

Artemis sat back in her chair, taking in the information. Benjamin's admission wasn't a surprise to her, but she needed to know more.

"Why do you still attend the groups?" she asked, her voice soft.

Benjamin shifted in his seat, his eyes darting around the room as if trying to find a way out.

"I just... I don't know. It helps, I guess. Being around people who understand."

Artemis nodded. "Understand what, exactly?"

"The struggle," Benjamin said, his voice barely above a whisper. "The addiction. It's not something you can just shake off. Even when you're not using, it's always there, lurking in the back of your mind."

Artemis leaned forward, her eyes boring into his. "Do you think someone in your group could be responsible for these murders?"

Benjamin shook his head vehemently. "No, no way. We're all just trying to get better."

Artemis didn't believe him, but she decided to let it go for now. There was something else she needed to know.

"What about your sister?" she asked, watching as Benjamin's face crumpled. "Does she know?"

"No!" he said, his voice sharp now. "Please don't tell her. She thinks too highly of me. She's... she's just... better than me."

His voice shook, and he stared at the table.

"Are you afraid of what she might say?" Artemis asked.

"Is it relevant?"

"Fear," she said simply. "Fear weakens the mind. It's an entry point for a hypnotist to exploit. You seem afraid of your sister finding out. She doesn't understand, then?"

He hesitated, his lips trembling. "No, no, she doesn't," he finally said. "She's always been... straight-laced, I guess you could say. She doesn't even like to drink."

Artemis didn't miss the way Benjamin's eyes flicked towards the door again, and she realized that he was worried about his sister hearing any of the conversation.

So she tried a different question. "Does Leo Ramirez attend the group?"

"Wh-who?"

"Leo," she said quietly.

"I don't know any Leo," he returned.

She frowned, feeling a jolt of frustration. She was banking on Ramirez being in the group as well. Still, she didn't give up just yet.

She said, "What about Javail Lillard?"

He suddenly brightened. "Yeah, I know Jav. What about him?"

She blinked, feeling a cold tremor along her arms now. "You do?"

"For sure. Good guy. Say, actually, I heard he might be coming up here as well."

"To the vineyard? So you haven't heard?"

"Heard what?"

"Javail was here," she said softly. She paused, then instead of explaining what happened, she said, "Where does your group meet, Benjamin?"

He scratched at his knuckles, the handcuffs shifting on the table.

"Not far from here. It's in the basement of St. Mark's church on Main Street. We meet on Thursdays, but they have a group on Sundays also."

Artemis felt a chill. "So they're meeting tonight?"

"Yeah. I guess so."

"And there's a second group?"

"I mean... some of the regulars attend both, but I didn't have time for that."

Artemis was now rubbing her hands together, feeling her excitement rising. If Leo Ramirez had attended the *second* group, then maybe she'd finally found her connection to it all.

Artemis nodded slowly, feeling her mind race with new possibilities. She needed to investigate this group further, and the meeting tonight seemed like a good start.

"Thank you, Benjamin," she said, standing up from her chair. "That's all for now. I'll have an officer come in to take you back to your cell. Stay strong." She met his gaze, nodding firmly. Again, she thought of her sister. Of how Dr. Bryant was taking all of this. Artemis' heart panged, and her tone communicated support as she said, "I'll make sure to do everything I can to clear your name. To help you."

He looked at her, then shrugged. "I did it. I killed her. You can't change that."

Artemis frowned briefly. Pausing. She swallowed. "You weren't in your right mind," she said.

His shoulders were slumped.

"It doesn't matter," he whispered. "Everything I love was taken away. I killed it."

Artemis stared at him, and she thought of her own sister once more. Helen had left in order to protect her family. Helen had killed others, too.

But no. Not Helen.

The Ghost Killer.

They were different. It wasn't Helen's fault.

Artemis frowned, and said, as fiercely as she could muster, "It wasn't your fault. Your sister needs you. I'm really, really sorry for what happened. Really. But don't give in to despair. It would crush Miracle. She loves you. I'm sure others do too. Please. If not for her sake, for yours. Don't give up."

She turned without waiting for a response, her hands shaking badly.

As she left the room, she couldn't shake the feeling that she was getting closer to the source of all of this. But with each step forward, she also felt herself getting deeper into a dangerous game.

And it all led back to a church's basement and a support group.

She paused by the second door in the hall, peering inside.

Forester was still interrogating Georgie and Lucas, but judging by his slumped posture through the window, things weren't going well.

She didn't have time to wait, though. It was almost evening.

She couldn't back down now. Not when she was so close.

With a deep breath, she continued down the hallway, determined to find the murderer. She would be safe, cautious.

She wouldn't show her hand.

Then, if she confirmed it, she'd call in backup and let them arrest the killer.

She nodded in determination and redoubled her speed down the hall, moving fast.

CHAPTER 27

Artemis moved cautiously, approaching the small church at the end of the street. Evening had come swiftly, and she was shivering from the chill breeze rushing down the slopes of the mountains and carrying the fragrance of fresh foliage across the street.

Her hands jammed in her pockets, and her oversized sweater bunched where she pressed her arms tight against her body, making herself as small as possible.

She shot a nervous look over her shoulder, down the street.

A street light was out above where she'd parked. Another light, further down, sputtered and occasionally illuminated a couple of men standing on a street corner.

Two figures were on the other side of the street, in an alley, and having a fierce conversation, complete with wild gesticulations.

Piles of trash littered the ground.

Artemis turned, hurrying towards the small church. An orange light extended from within, warming the concrete slab steps leading up to the front door.

She paused, reading a small sign.

Addicted? Jesus came to set you free!

She stared at the small graphic of a cartoon heart under which a light glowed out.

It was cheesy, but well-meaning. Still, she had to keep her guard up.

She paused on the stairs and stepped aside as a woman moved past her. The woman had dreadlocks and sunken eyes.

She flashed Artemis a quick smile, then pushed into the building, hastening into the illuminated halls.

Artemis followed at a respectable distance. They moved down a set of stairs, along a gray corridor towards what looked like an auditorium in the basement.

Voices were coming from within, complete with quiet chatter.

Artemis took a deep breath and pushed open the door. The room was dimly lit, filled with a variety of people. There were men and women, old and young, all speaking in hushed tones.

Artemis took a seat among them, her hands trembling slightly as she clasped them together.

A voice suddenly sounded from her side.

She glanced over.

A man was smiling at her. He had kind eyes and was wearing a thin fleece. "First time?" he said.

She shifted in the chair, hesitated as if unsure he'd been addressing her, then nodded. "Yeah. Yeah, I haven't been before."

He smiled, teeth flashing. "Well... there's always a first time for everything. Trust me," he said, in a low, conspiratorial whisper. "Things aren't as scary as they look." He gave her a quick encouraging nod, then returned to his conversation with the man at his side.

This second fellow was far more surly than the first. He was wide and barely fit in the provided folding chair.

He had a bald head and a thick beard, the hair on his arms and chest visible through the rips in his sleeveless shirt.

Artemis couldn't help but stare at him, wondering what brought him to this place.

As if sensing her gaze, the man turned to her and grinned, revealing a set of yellowed teeth. "Don't worry," he said, his voice a low rumble. "We're all here for the same reason."

Artemis didn't respond, still feeling uneasy. She glanced around the room, taking in the faces of those around her. Some looked lost and broken, while others were more composed, their eyes determined.

Suddenly, the lights dimmed further, and a man walked onto the small stage at the front of the room. He was tall and slender, with piercing blue eyes and a neatly trimmed mustache.

"Welcome," he said, his voice carrying a note of authority. "My name is Pastor Elijah, and I am here to help you find your way towards freedom."

Artemis leaned forward, her interest piqued. She had no idea what to expect, but the man on the stage commanded authority. He was smiling, and he also had long hair pulled back in a pony-tail. Pale skin, too, just like the description her father had elicited.

The pastor continued to speak, his words like a soothing balm. "Freedom isn't easy," he was saying. "Everyone has troubles. No one is perfect. Remember that when shame or guilt come knocking! Who the son sets free is free indeed, though. And I *promise* you," he said, flashing a winning smile. "You will be free."

She glanced around the room. People were hanging on to his words. Some leaned forward a bit. Some had wide eyes as they watched him, wearing hopeful expressions.

For her part, Artemis watched his posture. Poised, composed.

Was this the hypnotist? Should she call Forester?

There was no way for her to know just yet.

She needed to find out.

"We'll mingle for another fifteen minutes," the pastor was saying. "And then we can get started. We're just waiting on a couple more." He flashed another smile.

She wondered if he meant it to be warm and inviting. Really, it just felt practiced.

She thought of Dr. Bryant. The woman was also the sort to attend church, but she was different, somehow. There was an authenticity to Miracle that Artemis didn't always sense from people of the cloth.

Perhaps, though, she was being judgmental. Artemis wrinkled her brow, trying to refocus.

The whispered conversations continued. The pastor had stepped off the stage now and was beckoning to someone.

A young man.

The man was fidgeting nervously, but at the gesture from the pastor, he brightened and hastened over.

The two of them held a whispered conversation and then moved off behind the stage, disappearing into a back room.

Artemis stared.

The kind-eyed man at her side leaned in, and he adjusted his baseball cap, tilting it up. "Sometimes the pastor does private sessions before the meeting."

She glanced at the man, forced a quick smile, and nodded. The second, surly-faced, man with the paunch was sneezing, watering his eyes, and muttering, "Damn cats."

Artemis pushed from her chair, giving a polite nod to the friendly group attendee, and moving towards the door behind the stage.

What if the pastor was singling young men out in order to turn them into weapons? The way Leo and Benjamin had been honed?

She shivered, picking up her pace, feet tapping against the floor, moving away from the circle of chatter behind her.

She approached the door in the back of the stage and peered through.

She shot a quick glance over her shoulder to see if anyone was watching.

Only the man in the baseball cap with the kind eyes was looking her direction. He wasn't bad-looking, and she wondered if he was trying to hit on her.

She sighed but gave a quick, polite wave then pushed through the door into the hall behind the stage.

The door swung shut behind her, leaving her in a darkened space.

She waited, listening.

Voices at the end of the hall, coming from a closed door. Slow, steady voices. The voice of someone trying to establish a lulling rhythm?

She shivered, again wondering if she ought to call Forester now...

But time was of the essence. She was following a hunch, but that didn't mean she was right. Forester was still interrogating the brothers.

No... No, she'd call him when she had something concrete.

She wasn't going to confront anyone. Just watch, listen.

She paused, realizing that part of this newfound independence was to prove to herself she could.

The FBI field test was coming up.

She frowned slightly and then moved down the dingy hall towards the door with the voices.

As she approached, Artemis could hear the voice of Pastor Elijah speaking in soothing tones. He was alone with the young man she had seen him beckon earlier. Artemis hesitated for a moment, unsure of what to do. She knew that she was playing with fire by being here, but she couldn't shake the feeling that the connection between Benjamin and Leo wasn't for nothing.

She pressed her ear to the door and strained to hear what was being said. The young man was sobbing softly, and the pastor's voice was low and comforting. "It's okay, son," he was saying. "You're safe here. Confess your sins, and he will be faithful and just to forgive us our sins and cleanse us from all unrighteousness."

275

She frowned.

She pushed the door open a crack and peered inside. The room was dimly lit, with candles burning on a small altar in the corner. The young man was sitting in a chair, his head in his hands as he wept. The pastor was standing over him, his hand resting gently on the young man's shoulder.

Artemis could feel her heart pounding in her chest. The pastor handed a tissue to the young man and then removed contact with his hand, moved to a humble table of plywood and naked screws, and sat down again.

He was shaking his head. "We can come to your mother together, Maurice. I can be there if you want. But you need to tell her yourself. It's part of being a man. I believe in you."

She watched, feeling shivers along her back.

Maurice looked up, horrified. "No! No, she can't know. She'll kill me! She'll kick me out!"

The pastor sighed, massaging the bridge of his nose. And for a moment, the act from the stage faded. The performance disappeared.

But what she saw underneath wasn't a manipulative sadist. It wasn't some control freak.

It was an exhausted, weary man.

She'd never seen such exhaustion weighing down on a person before.

She stared.

Maurice didn't see it. He was still sitting in the chair, crying, protesting.

But she saw it.

She watched as the pastor summoned some hidden depth of resolve. He straightened a bit. The exhaustion from his eyes didn't vanish but seemed to diminish.

He hesitated, as if growing in strength, and then said, quietly, "I can find you a room here for a couple of months if it comes to that. You'll have to work. Clean the halls or help with the youth group."

Maurice froze, staring. "You'd... you'd let me help with the youth group? After what I just told you?"

The pastor smiled now, shaking his head, still weary. This time, the smile seemed genuine. It wasn't a stage smile.

The man said, "We all come from dark places, Maurice. I used to be an addict too."

"You don't call yourself an addict anymore?"

"Sometimes I wonder if I ever should've," the pastor said with a shrug. "I call myself redeemed, Maurice. I call myself free. But you need to tell your mother. Tell her how you've been making that money. Am I clear? Don't come back until you do. If she kicks you out, I'll make up a private room for you here. It's not much, but it's a place to sleep."

Artemis just watched, feeling an uncertainty returning. What was she missing?

This didn't seem like some bastard trying to entice someone to kill another.

Besides, all this talk of living with his mother... Maurice didn't seem like he had a spouse.

Not the target type.

She felt a little guilty now, too. She'd found herself judging the pastor's performance... But the man just seemed like he was tired and trying.

Sometimes that's all a soul could do. Try.

So what had she missed?

Artemis eased the door slowly shut, turning slightly.

And that's when she spotted the two figures at the end of the hall.

Moving slowly, in the opposite direction, heading towards a glowing red *Exit* sign.

It was the two men she'd seen before. The kind-eyed one with the baseball cap.

And the surly one with the paunch.

She stared, frozen in place.

The man with the cap had removed his hat, and now she spotted shoulder-length, pale hair.

He sauntered forward, and one arm wrapped around the shoulders of the second gentleman.

"Damn cats," the second guy was saying, and he continued to sniffle, rubbing at his nose.

Artemis stared and watched as the man with the cap brushed at his shoulder. "Sorry... Just a bit of fur."

A few strands of fur fell from his shoulder, fluttering to the ground.

Cat fur?

Or something else?

What about a wolf?

A wolf in sheep's clothing.

Neither man seemed to notice her watching.

They reached the exit.

The one with the pale hair and fur-covered shirt, said, "I appreciate you taking me up on this, Don. Trust me, I know how to help people like you."

"Shit, Gary... I hope so. I really do love her. She's just... so hard to please."

The man named Gary flashed a toothy smile. His kind eyes fixated on Don's downturned visage.

"Just trust me. I can help better than this place can. Let's hurry. We don't want to waste any time."

They pushed through the Exit, and Artemis' felt her blood go cold staring after them.

CHAPTER 28

She was racing down the hall now, phone in hand.

"Forester!" she was shouting into the receiver. "I found him. I found the killer! He's here!"

"Wait, you're sure?"

"Pretty damn. Shit. He's getting in a car. Dammit. Dammit!" her voice grew louder as she hurried from the alley exit, racing towards her own vehicle.

"Track the phone!" she yelled, leaving it on, but then stowing it in her pocket so she could snatch the keys.

She was *not* the type to drive. In fact, she hated driving.

She certainly hated the thought of high-speed chases.

But right now, the killer was getting away.

It all added up.

He fit the physical description. He had access to the group where the victims met.

He had fur on his shirt.

She knew it was him.

And now he was leading a man away who loved his wife.

It all fit. It was him.

She watched in horror as a Cadillac pulled from the church parking lot, veering onto a road and picking up speed. The brake lights glared back at her like red, demon eyes.

She slipped into her own car, gunned the engine, and raced after the car ahead of her.

She couldn't let him get away.

There was no telling what he might do to Don.

She spotted both figures in the front seat now, both sitting upright. The Cadillac was picking up speed, now, though. It merged onto a highway, circling a roundabout.

"Shit," she muttered.

The roundabout was too obvious. He'd spot her for sure, but she couldn't lose him.

She cursed again, feeling anxiety settle in her gut like a stone, and she took the ramp as well, trying to keep a healthy distance between their cars.

That's when he bolted.

He accelerated rapidly, veering into the left lane, and moving around other cars.

Horns honked, tires screeched.

"He spotted me!" she shouted, hoping Forester was still listening on the open line in her pocket.

It took her a second to summon inner resolve. She felt as if her anxiety was going to twist in her stomach like a knife. But then, exhaling deeply, summoning her courage, she floored the pedal, cursing under her breath and even offering up a small prayer, thanks in part to the church's effect.

Still, Jesus wouldn't take *this* wheel—and if she wasn't careful, she would careen into the semi-truck ahead of her.

She gritted her teeth so tightly, she thought something might crack, and her fingers trembled where they clutched at the steering wheel.

As she weaved in and out of traffic, the Cadillac just ahead of her, she could feel her pulse pounding in her temples. Her heart was racing, and adrenaline was coursing through her veins. She could see the driver of the Cadillac glancing in his rearview mirror, his face twisted with anger and frustration. The kind-eyes were gone, a mask slipping away.

But unlike the pastor, underneath the performance, there wasn't exhaustion. There was hatred.

He knew she was following him, and he was doing everything in his power to shake her off his tail.

But she wasn't about to let him get away. Not after all the time she had spent trying to track him down. Not after all the victims he had left in his wake. Miracle needed her brother. She needed to clear Benjamin's name.

Artemis swerved around a slow-moving sedan, her tires screeching as she took the turn too quickly. The Cadillac was just ahead of her, its taillights glowing like angry red eyes. She could hear the roar of its engine, and she knew that it was trying to put as much distance between them as possible.

But she wasn't going to give up. Her anxiety was still rising. If she had an anxiety attack on the highway, who knew how it would end.

But if she let the killer get away, then his passenger was in deep danger.

As they raced down the highway, she could see the lights of the city looming up ahead. She knew that the killer was trying to get lost in the crowd, to disappear into the night. But she wasn't going to let that happen.

With a fierce determination, she pushed her foot down on the accelerator, her car surging forward as she closed the distance between them. The Cadillac was just ahead of her now, its driver frantically trying to shake her off his tail.

She couldn't let him reach the city.

Couldn't let him have space to dispose of any evidence.

Or any witnesses.

"Come on!" she shouted. "Come on!"

Her mind fluttered. Briefly, she wondered what would Forester do?

The realization struck her and formed a pit in her stomach.

They were drawing near an off-ramp now. The tires squealed, the engine groaned.

"Dammit!" she yelled, realizing what she had to do.

She veered around the car, and it swerved as well, but then she redirected, slamming the front bumper into his rear bumper.

There was the screech of metal, the thud of collision and she rocked forward in her seat, the belt biting into her chest, her hands bruised on the firm wheel.

As the Cadillac spun out of control, Artemis slammed on the brakes, her car skidding to a stop just in time to avoid a head-on collision. The killer's car careened off the side of the road, smashing into a tree with a sickening crunch. Artemis sat frozen for a moment, her heart pounding in her chest as she tried to process what had just happened.

Finally, she forced herself to move, unbuckling her seatbelt and stumbling out of the car. She could hear the sound of sirens in the distance, growing louder by the second.

With a deep breath, she approached the wrecked Cadillac, her hands trembling. The driver's side door was hanging off its hinges, and she could see the killer slumped over the steering wheel, blood dripping from a gash on his forehead.

Artemis approached cautiously, her heart in her throat. She had no idea if the killer was still alive or if he was armed. But as she got closer, she could see that he was unconscious, his breath coming in shallow gasps.

She reached into the car and checked his pulse, relieved to find that he was still alive. She knew she had to act fast, though.

With a grunt of effort, she pulled the killer out of the car and dragged him to the side of the road.

She then raced back, hastening to the other side door where Don had been sitting.

Except he wasn't there.

She stared into the car, hesitant.

She paused only briefly, then heard a crunch behind her.

The sound of a foot against sticks.

A horrible thought suddenly struck her.

And then a branch did the same. Her head exploded in pain, and she stumbled forward.

Black spots danced across her vision.

It took her a second to realize she was on the ground, hands braced against the detritus, inhaling the scent of mold and moss and leaves.

She couldn't move.

Her mind was a jumbled mess. Thoughts came slowly.

Two of them.

The two of them were in on it together. They had tricked her. They'd known who she was—maybe had seen her at the resort.

They'd lured her.

Then something struck her again, and darkness came quick.

CHAPTER 29

Artemis' eyes fluttered, and pain lanced through her head. She woke slowly and tried to move.

But couldn't.

She grimaced, and her memories came back. She'd been ambushed.

Tricked.

Blood now rushed to her face. Her heart twisted in her chest. She tried to move again and, with horror, realized she was tied to a chair.

She blinked a few more times...

And that's when she heard the growling sound. An absolutely gigantic, lupine creature was sitting by a fireplace across from her.

This one, unlike the last wolf she'd encountered, had no chain.

It was sitting there, watching her with golden eyes. She tried to move again, but her bonds were too strong.

Her breath was coming in quick gasps. Anxiety was now tearing through her like hot needles.

She could barely think straight. It felt as if she were stuck on a roller-coaster, her heart leaping into her throat then plummeting into her feet as a panic attack began to take hold.

And then she heard the voice.

In most contexts, it might have been described as a soothing voice.

But now, it sent shivers down her spine.

"Well you really have been a bother, haven't you?"

Artemis' eyes adjusted to the light. The room was flickering, and she realized this was due to the fireplace casting a glow across the room.

The wolf was growling in the corner, and she shot it another frightened look.

"Don't worry," said the man who'd given his name as Gary. He was smiling now, and his shoulder-length hair was brushed behind his ears. "He won't attack you until I tell him to."

The word *until* really stuck out to her.

Her eyes fluttered, and her head ached. She shifted uncomfortably in her seat, glancing down through blinking eyes at the way her hands were bound.

She looked past Gary and spotted his compatriot standing there as well.

Don didn't look nearly as sad now, but he still had a surly expression. He was about a foot taller than Gary and rested his hand on his shoulder.

"You two are lovers?" she asked quietly, staring at the men.

The pale-faced man with shoulder-length hair sneered at her. "You don't know us. You don't know anything. You're just like her aren't you?"

Artemis paused. "You mean your wife? The one you killed?"

He blinked.

Don went still.

They both stared at her.

It wasn't a lucky guess, more like an educated deduction.

She'd spotted the outline around his finger of a tan mark that had never quite healed. A ring removed.

Plus, he'd been luring men to kill their wives.

It was a guess but confirmed by their reaction.

She knew she needed to stall. The wolf was still growling by the fireplace, and she refused to look in its direction.

Quickly, she said, "We've been onto you for a while. No sense racking up another murder charge. We know what you've done."

"I never killed my wife," he said simply. "She killed herself. She jumped to her death." Then, his lips twisted. "You think you're clever, don't you?"

He was leaning forward now, his hands pressed tight against his lap. One of the hands was tapping rhythmically.

She shivered. "I'm sorry for your loss. But we know all about it."

She winced, grimacing as the ropes bit into her hands again.

"I think you're lying," he sneered. "I saw you at the vineyard. You and your boyfriend." He smirked. "Handsome fella, wasn't he? Pity you're going out the way you are."

Artemis shook her head. "It doesn't have to be like this."

"I can smell your fear, girl. I know what you are. Recently broken up, aren't you? This new guy is a fling."

Artemis stared back at him but covered just as quickly, shaking her head. "Fish all you want," she murmured.

But he smiled, his lips twisting. "I'm right. You're not a Fed. You're training to be one. You love your mother but hate your father."

He was right about the training part but completely off on the family part. She'd never known her mother.

She felt a shiver. He wasn't as good as her dad. No one was, but he was good. She had to hand it to him.

She felt as if she were locked into a mental chess match, but it also felt like Zugzwang.

The position in a match where defeat was imminent.

She was tied to the furniture, unable to move.

Now, the man was waving his hand. "Normally," he said, "I'd play some games. Maybe get you to kill yourself, but we're in a bit of a hurry, I'm afraid. So..." he shrugged. "I haven't fed my pet tonight. I hope you don't mind."

He began to turn now, moving towards the door. He raised his hands above his head as if to click his fingers.

The wolf perked up at the gesture, leaning forward as if preparing to rush Artemis at the moment the man clicked his fingers.

Desperation flared through her. "Wait!" she screamed. "You have to tell me. Why? Why kill them?"

He paused, his hand still raised, but he turned, glancing back at her, an amused smirk on his features.

"Really? Stalling? To what end, girl?"

His tall companion behind him was chuckling now. Both staring at her.

She shivered horribly. "I... I don't... Please!" she said, her voice shaking.

She was pleading. Not because she thought it would help, but because it was what someone like this wanted. He enjoyed the power. Enjoyed the control, the groveling.

"I... I'm scared," she whimpered. "Please!"

"Oh, cut it out," he snapped. "Who do you think you're fooling?"

She just shook her head, still crying. "Oh, God... please!"

He watched her, curious, something aroused in his eyes. He liked what he was seeing. Most psychopaths couldn't help themselves. He smoothly stroked at his knuckles, and the wolf was still perked up, still attentive.

Artemis needed to stall. Just a bit longer.

She could feel the phone pressed against her leg. Was it still on?

Had Forester managed to track her?

It was the only play she had.

To stall for time.

To stall until Forester could arrive with backup.

But the wolf was so close.

The man was going to leave the room.

She had to do something... but what? Offer something he'd want to hear. Something that would actually interest a man like this.

"You're a killer. A hypnotist," she said quietly.

"Obviously." He began to turn again.

"You know my father, don't you?"

He paused, glancing back at her. "The Ghost Killer," she said simply.

It was the only card she could think to play. A killer who operated in the Seattle area as a mentalist would definitely know about Otto Blythe.

He blinked, staring at her.

And then, his hand lowered slightly. He let out a giddy little laugh. "I *knew* I recognized you. Don, shit, it's Artemis Blythe. From the news!"

Both men were now staring at her as if they'd just run into a favorite celebrity.

Artemis remained rigid in the seat, trying to keep her expression friendly, earnest.

Gary was laughing now, shaking his head. "Your father was an inspiration to me. He got caught, though," he added. Snorting now. He sighed and shrugged once more. "Pity. But daddy issues or not, you've seen too much. And I, for one, don't want to be caught."

He turned again.

She was out of time. She needed *something* to distract him. Anything.

So she blurted out, "My father's innocent, you know. He didn't do it. I know the real Ghost Killer."

The man in the door paused again, not looking back at her this time. He had tensed.

The wolf seemed to sense its master's mood, and leaned forward, panting heavily now.

Artemis could hear droplets of saliva tapping against the floor as the sparks hissed behind the beast from the fireplace.

"You're still stalling," the man said quietly. "I just can't help but wonder why."

"Would you like to speak with him?" she said quickly. "I have his number. You can talk to my father yourself."

Gary turned again, watching her sharply now.

He licked his lips briefly.

She tried to force a smile.

Don was now frowning, though. "Forget it, Gar. She's wasting time. Let's get out of here."

"It wouldn't take long. When's the last time you had a chance to speak with the Ghost Killer?"

"I thought you said he wasn't?"

"I thought you said you didn't believe me?"

Time was passing. But not much. How long until Forester arrived? Was her phone even on?

Had she made a mistake?

Don kept tugging at Gary's arm, trying to pull him back now. The larger man was glaring at Artemis with an expression of severe distrust.

Artemis could sense the tension in the room, and her heart was racing with fear. She had to keep stalling until Forester arrived, but she was running out of ideas. Gary was still watching her, his eyes flickering with interest.

"You really know the Ghost Killer?" he asked, his voice low and dangerous.

Artemis nodded quickly. "Yes, I do. He's not the person you think he is. Why don't you just give him a call?"

Gary's eyes narrowed, and his hand moved towards the wolf as if gesturing for it to approach. "I don't believe you," he said, his voice cold. "But maybe we can find out the truth together. Pain loosens lips. My ex-wife used to say that." He smirked at her.

Artemis felt a cold sweat break out on her forehead. She had to come up with something fast.

"Wait," she pleaded.

But he didn't seem to care.

"No more stalling," he snapped. He moved towards the door and stepped through. His partner followed him.

Then, Gary turned back, glared at her, and raised his hand. "Good-bye."

He snapped his fingers.

And slammed the door.

Artemis was now locked, alone, in the room with the wolf.

And at the sound of the snapping fingers, she heard the beast howl. Out of the corner of her eye, where she'd tried not to look in its direction, the beast lunged at her, teeth bared.

CHAPTER 30

Artemis did the only thing she could think of, and she knew it would hurt.

She pivoted.

Her hands were bound. Her legs bound. But her feet were loose, pressed to the floor. She was able to shift the chair, only slightly but enough to temporarily protect her back from the wolf's jaws, presenting the backrest to it.

The wolf careened into the chair, sending it toppling to the floor, Artemis with it.

As she'd hoped, the weight of the wolf, the sudden collision, it shattered the armrests.

She managed to pull her arms free, but her legs were still tied to the wooden chair.

She screamed, trying to keep the splintered backrest between her and the beast.

Using the slatted wood as something of a shield.

The creature kept swiping at her, snarling, its claws raking into the temporary, wooden shield.

It tried to bite at her fingers and cut through one.

Blood welled up along her right hand.

She was scrambling back now, desperate, trying to keep the wolf off her.

Artemis managed to shake one leg free now that the ropes had loosened from the broken chair. The chair leg had come off but was still secured against her leg.

She managed to reach her feet, stumbling, still keeping the remnants of the chair between her and the monster.

It stalked towards her now, slower, slobbering, eyes hooded.

It knew she had nowhere to go.

And then, as fast as thought, it launched at her again.

She screamed as the wolf lunged at her, its hot breath hitting her face. She scrambled back again, this time putting the table between her and the beast.

It was ripping the backrest to shreds from where it had pulled it from her hands.

It now snarled as it spat splinters and looked over at where she was cowering behind the table.

She looked around frantically, trying to find a way out, but the windows were too high to reach and the door was shut. She'd heard them lock it.

She backed away from the wolf, her eyes fixed on its bared teeth. She needed a weapon, something to defend herself with. She spotted the wooden chair leg still tied to her own leg. She gasped, reached down, fingers fumbling, and tugged. Her hand was still bleeding, but she managed to pull the chair leg free, holding it up like a club.

The wolf growled, its eyes fixed on the club. It circled her, keeping its distance, and trying to edge around the table. Artemis held the club tightly, her heart pounding in her chest. She had to find a way out of this room before it was too late.

But the wolf was preparing to lunge again. She could feel it bracing itself. She glanced under the table.

An opening there, and a gap beneath the opening.

The table was low to the ground, with a knee space as large as she was. And under the knee space, about a foot of open air.

A thought formulated.

It was a risky move.

But it would have to work.

"Come on," she yelled at the wolf. "Come and get me!"

It obliged, pouncing at her once more, claws flashing.

She dove under the table.

It came after her.

But she wasn't trying to hide in the knee space.

Rather, she went flat, prone, dragging herself along the ground to fit *under* the foot-tall gap.

She was thin, small.

She managed to squeeze through, then felt teeth bite into her leg.

She screamed in pain but kicked out.

Her leg ripped free, blood pouring now. Pain lancing through her, carried by adrenaline.

But she kept moving.

She slipped out from under the desk.

The wolf's jaws tried to follow her, teeth stained in red.

But now, it was trapped under the desk.

So she shoved it.

The thing was too large to fit under the foot-sized gap.

Its own size was now its greatest weakness.

She flung her small frame against the desk, shoving it against the wall.

Now, the knee space was blocked by the wall, and the foot-tall gap was too thin for the wolf to exit.

She'd essentially trapped it under the desk, between the wall, in a small box of wood.

The wolf howled, the desk shuddering.

It was trying to shove off the wall now, but the concrete had no give.

She gasped, leaning against the desk, keeping it lodged against the wall.

She was bleeding from her leg.

Her hand.

She heard commotion now, above her.

The sound of footsteps. Shouting.

Then sirens.

Gunshots.

She froze.

More gunshots.

The wolf went quiet, frightened. It let out a whimpering sound.

Suddenly, she heard the sound of footsteps outside the door. She turned towards the door, her heart racing.

"Artemis!" she heard Forester's voice calling out to her. "Are you in there?"

Another gunshot.

The door handle exploded inward.

Artemis ran towards the door, holding the club tightly. She heard the wolf behind her, the desk scraping now that she wasn't holding it closed.

The beast's paws hit the floor as it charged after her.

"Artemis!" Forester shouted.

She lunged through the open door.

"CLOSE IT!" she screamed.

Forester didn't hesitate. He slammed the door shut with his shoulder.

And they both went completely still, breathing heavily, standing in the hall, staring towards the sealed door.

The beast was still snarling, gasping, growling.

Artemis was still frozen in place, fear pounding through her.

Forester held the door shut, wrapping one arm around her. "Hang tight. You're hurt."

"I'm fine," she said weakly. "Two of them. Two."

"We got 'em. Both. They shot each other."

She stared. "They killed themselves?"

"Yeah. Yeah... Thank God you're alive."

She winced, nodding slowly.

He gave her another quick side hug.

Then, his face paled as he saw her leg, her hand. "We need to get you some help."

"It'll be fine."

"Now!"

She could feel her vision threatening to fade.

So she nodded, breathing slowly.

And Cameron grabbed the wooden chair leg from her, using it to block the door.

Behind him, she spotted three more police racing down a set of stairs. "Don't go in there!" Cameron snapped.

This time, she noticed how he had no apparent concern for the wolf.

He was consistent in this way. His compassion only went so far... until she was threatened.

Her father had once told her that he knew Forester's secret.

But he'd never told her what.

Now, as he hastily led her away, she found she didn't much care.

Her eyes were growing dark. Her mind was spinning, and she followed after Cameron as he allowed her to lean on him, guiding her limping form through a dark hall and towards the light.

EPILOGUE

Artemis sat in the hospital bed, watching the television play a re-run of the latest tournament she'd missed.

She was slipping in the rankings while absent.

She frowned at the screen, sitting up, back against a set of pillows.

The hospital room was empty, quiet at midnight.

She stared across the room at the television, watching as Hakaru Fedelson began the match with D4.

"You wuss," she muttered under her breath, watching as the black pieces responded with D5.

She shook her head, closing her eyes and relaxing as best she could.

The case was solved.

Both the killers had shot themselves.

Benjamin Clarkson was going to treatment rather than prison.

She allowed herself a faint smile.

And then the door to the hospital room opened.

She turned, staring. Her heart hammered.

It wasn't Forester, though. She still wasn't sure how she was supposed to deal with that man.

She'd made up her mind, though. She'd have to talk. Have to tell him the truth.

No matter what... he deserved the truth.

The thought alone sent shivers through her. But this case... this experience had proven one thing. Helen could be helped. Artemis could help her sister. It was time to return home.

And now, a piece of home had emerged in the hospital room.

It was her father.

He stood there, watching her, a look of concern in his eyes.

He was still wearing his disguise, and in the dark, he looked like a stranger.

Except for his eyes. She recognized those familiar, pale blue eyes.

"Artemis," he said softly.

She blinked. "How'd you get in here?"

"I have my ways." He looked at her bandaged leg. "Are you okay?"

She nodded. "I'm fine. It's just a few scrapes and bruises."

He nodded. "Good. Good."

He stepped closer. "I... I was scared I'd lost you."

She watched him, hesitant.

He shook his head. "Really scared, Artemis."

"I'm sorry," she whispered.

"And I... I can't just stand by. Not now."

She hesitated, watching him. The pain in her leg was only a dull sensation now. The pain meds they'd given were working wonders.

But now, her system was on high alert.

Her father said, "I know you may be mad at me. But I have to tell you something."

She felt her heart thudding in her chest.

He swallowed. "I know you're mad at me for keeping secrets. But I'm not the only one."

Artemis felt her breath catch in her throat.

He continued. "You deserve to know. I... I'm sorry I didn't do a very good job. I should've kept you safe. All of you. And I'm promising you now, Artemis. I promise. I'll do everything I can to keep you together. To rebuild *us.* The Blythe family."

"That... that doesn't sound like a secret," she said. She even allowed a small ghost of a smile. "I'd like that. I think we all would. I know she can be helped, Dad. I *know* it."

"I believe you. I really do. But we can't have dangerous types around. Not with her. She's too fragile."

Artemis blinked. "What do you mean?"

He stared at her for a second, clearly hesitant, then all at once, he stepped forward and wrapped his arms around her. She stiffened but didn't recoil.

Neither did he.

It was an awkward hug. Not so much warm, or comforting as...

Necessary.

And she found her chest stirring. Emotions rising. Her eyes grew wet. She didn't cry, not fully. But felt herself welling up, finally allowing herself to feel, at least for a moment, the fear and sadness that had been building for so long.

They stayed there for a long moment, hugging.

When he finally stepped back, he was wiping his eyes. "I have to protect you. To protect us. Like I should've done."

"What are you talking about?" she asked, her voice a murmur now. Was it the pain medication?

But then, his next words caused her to sit up, alert.

He said, "It's about Cameron Forester. About what he did. Who he is."

She stared at her father.

"I found some things, Artemis. Terrible things." His voice was grim, and his eyes flashed as he looked at her. "Things you need to know."

What's Next for Artemis?

She Bleeds Slowly

Even billionaires bleed...

Ecola State Park is considered by many to be one of the most beautiful preserves in the country, surrounded by some of the wealthiest communities in the world. But amidst the scenic coastlines, and the hiking trails, the bodies of the wealthy and the elite are turning up dead.

Three wounds each, one for each comma in their bank accounts. Secret billionaire parties and tight-lipped communities stump genius chessmaster and FBI trainee Artemis Blythe; she fears she may have finally met her match.

The wealthy local communities blame the off-grid population known to be living in the state park, but Artemis isn't so sure. She thinks something far more nefarious is at foot.

Also by Georgia Wagner

The River's Secret

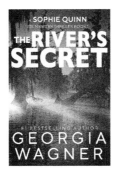

A cold knife, a brutal laugh.

Then the odds-defying escape.

Once a hypnotist with her own TV show, now, Sophie Quinn works as a full-time consultant for the FBI. Everything changed six years ago. She can still remember that horrible night. Slated to be the River

Killer's tenth victim, she managed to slip her bindings and barely escape where so many others failed. Her sister wasn't so lucky.

And now the killer is back.

Two PHDs later, she's now a rising star at the FBI. Her photographic memory helps solve crimes, but also helps her to never forget. She saw the River Killer's tattoo. She knows what he sounds like. And now, ten years later, he's active again.

Sophie Quinn heads back home to the swamps of Louisiana, along the Mississippi River, intent on evening the score and finding the man who killed her sister. It's been six years since she's been home, though. Broken relationships and shattered dreams exist among the bayous, the rivers, the waterways and swamps of Louisiana; can Sophie find her way home again? Or will she be the River Killer's next victim to float downstream?

Also by Georgia Wagner

Girl Under the Ice

Once a rising star in the FBI, with the best case closure rate of any investigator, Ella Porter is now exiled to a small gold mining town bordering the wilderness of Alaska. The reason for her new assignment? She allowed a prolific serial killer to escape custody.

But what no one knows is that she did it on purpose.

The day she shows up in Nome, bags still unpacked, the wife of the richest gold miner in town goes missing. This is the second woman to vanish in as many days. And it's up to Ella to find out what happened.

Assigning Ella to Nome is no accident, either. Though she swore she'd never return, Ella grew up in the small, gold mining town, treated like royalty as a child due to her own family's wealth. But like all gold tycoons, the Porter family secrets are as dark as Ella's own.

WANT TO KNOW MORE?

Greenfield press is the brainchild of bestselling author Steve Higgs. He specializes in writing fast paced adventurous mystery and urban fantasy with a humorous lilt. Having made his money publishing his own work, Steve went looking for a few 'special' authors whose work he believed in.

Georgia Wagner was the first of those, but to find out more and to be the first to hear about new releases and what is coming next, you can join the Facebook group by copying the following link into your browser - www.facebook.com/GreenfieldPress

ABOUT THE AUTHOR

Georgia Wagner worked as a ghost writer for many, many years before finally taking the plunge into self-publishing. Location and character are two big factors for Georgia, and getting those right allows the story to flow seamlessly onto the page. And flow it does, because Georgia is so prolific a new term is required to describe the rate at which nerve-tingling stories find their way into print.

When not found attached to a laptop, Georgia likes spending time in local arboretums, among the trees and ponds. An avid cultivator of orchids, begonias, and all things floral, Georgia also has a strong penchant for art, paintings, and sculptures. A many-decades long passion for mystery novels and years of chess tournament experience makes Georgia the perfect person to pen the Artemis Blythe series.

Printed in Great Britain
by Amazon